THE BUDDY BOOK

it's a God thing!

Other books in the Young Women of Faith Library

The Lily Series

Here's Lily

Lily Robbins, M.D. (Medical Dabbler)

Lily and the Creep

Lily's Ultimate Party

Non-fiction

The Beauty Book

The Best Bash Book

The Body Book

Dear Diary: A Girl's Book of Devotions

Girlz Want to Know: Answers to Real-Life Questions

Young Women of Faith

THE BUDDY BOOK

it's a God thing!

Written by Nancy Rue
Illustrated by Lyn Boyer

Zonderkidz

Zonderkidz™
The children's group of Zondervan

The Buddy Book

Requests for information should be addressed to:

Zonderkidz, *Grand Rapids, Michigan 49530*

www.zonderkidz.com

ISBN: 0-310-70064-7

Published in association with the literary agency of Alive Communications, Inc., 7680 Goddard Street, Suite 200, Colorado Springs, CO 80920.

Art direction and interior design by Michelle Lenger

Printed in the United States of America

01 02 03 04 05 /❖ DC/ 12 11 10 9 8 7 6 5 4 3 2

For *my* best buddy, Jimmy Rue

Contents

chapter
1

Relationships? Aren't Those Just for Adults?

"The second [commandment] is this: 'Love your neighbor as yourself.'"
(Mark 12:31)

Relationship? Isn't that something they talk about on soap operas and sitcoms?

The word *relationship* is all over the place these days. When you're flipping channels, you hear it at least three times a minute, on everything from talk shows to deodorant commercials. If you accidentally eavesdrop on one of your mom's phone conversations, relationships will come up at least once, whether she's talking about your dad, you, or the family *dog*. And if you're looking for something on the magazine table to save you from boredom at the dentist's office, just about every cover is going to beckon you with something about "relationships" featured inside—"How to Communicate with Your Kids," "How to Relate to Your Doctor," "How to Talk to Your Houseplants."

But even though that word—*relationships*—is everywhere, you might dismiss it whenever you see and hear it, because it sounds like some deep "thing" reserved for the adult world. Don't only grown-ups have relationships?

Okay, answer your own question. Do you:

- live alone?
- get your schooling strictly through a computer program—no teacher, no fellow students?
- spend all your free time completely by yourself?
- refuse to pray or read the Bible?

If you answered no to any of those questions, here's a news flash for you: You have relationships!

The concept isn't all that sophisticated. Your relationships are simply what happens between you and the other significant people in your life. You have relationships with the following people—and probably more:

- your parents or your legal guardians or maybe both
- your siblings (your brothers and sisters)
- any other relatives you hang with often
- your friends
- your teachers
- any other adults who are important to you—from your gymnastics coach to the driver who calls you "Blondie" every morning when you get on the bus

Your life is loaded with relationships. Unless you're quarantined, you can barely go for five minutes of your awake life without relating to somebody. In fact, you spend less time alone now than you ever will again after you get your driver's license!

Even when you are alone, you always have two other relationships going on:

- the one with yourself
- the one with God

You couldn't get away from relationships if you wanted to—and why would you want to? Relationships among people are, after all, a God-thing.

HOW IS THIS A God Thing?

Erase all the relationships from the Bible, and what do you have? Uh, the Garden of Eden . . . before Adam and Eve . . . and, uh . . . that's about it.

The Bible is loaded with important relationships that God created:

- God made Eve for Adam because "for Adam no suitable helper was found." (Genesis 2: 20)
- When God instructed Noah on building the ark, he told him to make rooms in it for his wife and his sons and his sons' wives. (Genesis 6:9–21)
- When God told Abram to leave his country, Abram didn't go alone; he took his wife Sarai and his nephew Lot with him. (Genesis 12:1–5)
- When Isaac's wife, Rebekah, couldn't have any children, God was the one who made it possible for her to have a baby. (Genesis 25:21)

That's only part of the first book of the Old Testament. When you get to the New Testament, Jesus talks almost nonstop about relationships.

He says:

"I tell you that anyone who is angry with his brother will be subject to judgment." ***(Matthew 5:22)***

"If your brother sins against you, go and show him his fault, just between the two of you." ***(Matthew 18:15)***

"Do to others as you would have them do to you." ***(Luke 6:31)***

"If [your brother] sins against you seven times in a day, and seven times comes back to you and says, 'I repent,' forgive him." ***(Luke 17:4)***

"Love each other as I have loved you." ***(John 15:12)***

"Greater love has no one than this, that he lay down his life for his friends." ***(John 15:13)***

The Gospels are like a self-help book about relationships written by God. Jesus covers it all—friends, enemies, parents, sisters and brothers—even your relationship with God and with yourself. Being a Christian is *all about* relationships, and it isn't too early in your life to make sure yours are in good shape.

What Happens If Your Relationships AREN'T Wonderful?

If your relationships with other people and with yourself and with God aren't so good, life can be miserable. We've all been there, so consider how you might answer these questions:

- Do you remember a time when you had a fight with your brother or sister? ("Do I remember *a* time? Do I have to pick just one? How about the one we had ten minutes ago?")
- Can you recall disagreeing with your parents about something? ("Only *one* something? How about practically everything!")

- Have you ever had a blow-up with your best friend? ("Uh, you mean, like we didn't speak to each other for two days, when usually we call each other up every two hours?")
- Have you ever done something you felt so bad about that you couldn't forget it? ("Like, I turn red every time I even think about it?")
- Was there a time when you got mad at God? ("Would that be the time when I sat in church with my arms folded and wouldn't sing any of the songs?")

If your answers were similar, you know what it's like when any of your relationships is in a funk. It's a complete bummer, and who wants to feel like that all the time? You don't have to, but having good relationships does take work. Otherwise, Jesus wouldn't have gone through all he did to come down here and show us how to get along with God, ourselves, and others!

That's what *The Buddy Book* is for—to help you understand what relationships are about, to let you explore your own love connections with your friends and family and make them easier and more fun, and to give you a peek at the kinds of relationships that are coming up for you as you grow up (and trust me, you'll never stop "growing up").

Let's start by seeing what shape your relationships are in right now.

✓ CHECK Yourself OUT

Here are some statements about—you guessed it—relationships, and below each one are some ways to finish those statements. Circle the letter of the "finisher" that is most like you.

1. **I have a disagreement with my parents**
   A. practically every day.
   B. maybe once a week or so.
   C. almost never, once a month at the most.

2. **When I do have a disagreement with my parents**
   A. we do a lot of yelling and screaming.
   B. I get resentful, but I get over it—until next time.
   C. we talk things over and get it worked out.

3. **I can talk to my parents about**
   A. nothing, because they just don't understand me.
   B. some things, but I don't tell them everything.
   C. everything, because they "get it".

4. **When it comes to hanging out and having a good time, my parents are**
   A. a drag; what's fun to me isn't fun to them.
   B. are a lot of fun some of the time; other times I'd rather be with my friends.
   C. are my favorite people to be with.

5. **My sibling(s) are**
   A. a pain.
   B. all right most of the time.
   C. very cool.

6. **I fight or argue with my siblings**
   A. constantly, at least once a day.
   B. fairly often, at least once a week.
   C. not much; I can hardly remember the last time we got into it.

7. **When it comes to friends**
   A. I feel like I don't have any, or not enough, anyway.
   B. I'm okay with them, but sometimes I'm still lonely.
   C. I have really neat friends, and just enough of them.

8. **My friends and I**
   A. get into a lot of fights; at least once a week we're going at it.

B. don't fight very much; maybe every couple of weeks we stop speaking to each other for an hour or so.

C. almost never fight—I can hardly even imagine us arguing.

9. I feel like my friends treat me

A. like dirt sometimes.

B. like somebody who has just always been there.

C. like I'm somebody special.

10. Boys are

A. pretty much gross and disgusting.

B. a little bit scary to me.

C. just like anybody else (and maybe even better at times).

11. Older people—like over thirty—

A. are boring, and I don't like hanging around them.

B. are sometimes okay, but I don't think of them as friends.

C. are a lot of times pretty cool, and I have some as friends.

12. If I met myself someplace for the first time, I would

A. run the other way.

B. maybe consider being friends.

C. jump at the chance to be friends.

13. God and I

A. don't speak to each other.

B. talk some, like at night when I go to bed and when I'm in church.

C. talk a lot; I think of God as being close to me.

Now go back and count how many A's you circled, how many B's, and how many C's. Write your numbers here: A ____ B ____ C____

Was your highest number for the C's? If so, that means you think your relationships are in good shape. Get a big grin on your face—you're on a roll! Read on, though, so you'll know how to keep them that way, especially with the changes that will surely happen in your life in the next couple of years. Pay extra careful attention in the chapters that deal with the areas you did mark A or B.

Was your highest number for the B's? If that's the case, you're feeling as if your relationships are okay but nothing to feature on the six o'clock news. You may want them to be better, more fun, or less hassle-filled. Reading *The Buddy Book* will help you start pumping up and smoothing out those relationships, especially the ones pertaining to areas you didn't mark with C's. Now's the perfect time to get working on those relationships, because the changes ahead in your teen years will be a lot easier if you have good relationships.

Was your highest number for the A's? If you answer yes, you're probably not really happy with your relationships. Don't beat yourself up over it! That happens, and the good news is that they can be fixed. Every chapter of *The Buddy Book* can help you. This is a great chance for you to change some things that are making your life less fun and more of a mess than it could be.

What Makes Any Relationship Good?

Before we go on to talk about different kinds of relationships, like the ones you have with your parents, your brothers and sisters, and your friends, let's talk about some basics that apply to all your friendships, from Dad to God. It's the kind of thing

Girlz WANT TO KNOW

✿ ***LILY: My brothers are always telling me I'm too bossy, and my best friend sometimes gets in my face about that too. But what am I supposed to do, be a doormat?***

Heavens, no! Don't be a rug people can walk on! Just be sure you know the difference between being bossy and being assertive. Being assertive means saying how you feel and what you want without expecting everybody to scurry around giving you your own way. Maybe an example will help:

Bossy: Go get your Monopoly game, and we'll play that.

Doormat: I don't care. Whatever you want to play is fine with me, as usual.

Assertive: I want to play Monopoly. What did you have in mind?

✿ ***SUZY: Nobody listens to me. It's like people don't even know I'm there half the time—including my parents! Do I have to be some loud-mouthed weirdo for people to hear what I have to say?***

Yikes, no! You don't ever have to change who you really are to get people to pay attention. The key is to let people see who you really are. Next time you're with other people—even your own family—ask yourself these questions:

- Am I looking people in the eye, or am I staring at the floor or the ceiling or darting my eyes all over the room?
- Am I sitting up straight and welcoming people with my posture, or are my shoulders all slumped down and my head hanging like I don't want anybody to listen to me?
- Am I speaking loud and clear, or am I mumbling into my lower lip like I don't want anybody to hear me?
- If somebody asks me a question, do I answer, or do I just shrug my shoulders and say, "Whatever"?

Not everybody can stand in the middle of a room and yell, "Hey, I wanna talk!" But everybody—including you—can be heard. It means practicing these things:

- Make eye contact with people. Eyes talk, and people will "hear" in your look that you have something to say.
- Sit up and look like you're following the conversation. When you cross your arms and look at people through your hair, they get the signal that you'd like to be left alone.

- When you do have something to say, go ahead and speak up. If you mutter, those people who can come into the room yelling, "Hey, I wanna talk!" won't even know you've opened your mouth! That doesn't mean you have to be loud and obnoxious. In fact, loud and obnoxious seldom gets people anywhere anyway. But do spit it right out. You'll be surprised at the results.
- If you get nervous about speaking up, try to relax. I know that's a lot like saying, "Try to be president of the United States," but it really can be done. Take a couple of deep breaths when you feel the butterflies starting to flit around in your stomach. That will keep you from getting into a knot about not being heard, and you can use your energy to speak up.
- Listen openly to what other people are saying. Ask them questions. Nod when you agree. Shake your head when you don't. That'll help you build up the courage to say, "Yeah!" or "No way!"

✿ ***ZOOEY: I hate it when people hurt my feelings, and it happens all the time—my parents, my teachers, even my friends. How can I get them to not be so mean to me?***

Actually there are two different things you can do:

1. When somebody says something that hurts you, instead of going off to the girls' bathroom to cry (that's always my first instinct!), go to that person and, as calmly as you can, tell him or her that you've been stung by what was said. Nothing can change if the person who hurts you doesn't even know he or she is doing it.
2. Think about whether it's really a big deal. Some hurts are a big deal, like if somebody calls you "Miss Piggy" or puts you down because you're a Baptist (or because you're not a Baptist). But other things you might be able to let go, such as, "That's a weird looking backpack, Zooey," or "My mother doesn't pack my lunch—I always buy." It's okay for people to have different tastes than yours. It's not okay for them to attack you personally.

✿ ***RENI: My dad really goes off on me sometimes over what I think are the stupidest things—like I didn't put the garbage can lid on right or***

something. He always comes back and apologizes later, but I don't always feel like forgiving him. Does that make me a bad person?

Nope, you're definitely not a bad person. You're a human person. It's natural for some of us to hold grudges we intend to keep a grip on until the Second Coming. But Jesus says we can't, so it looks like you're going to need to work on that. Try two things:

1. Ask your dad—or anyone else who "goes off" on you without a good reason—why he does that. Seeing it from his point of view might make it easier to forgive—particularly if he, say, has migraines or his work is driving him batty.
2. Pray for anyone you have a grudge against. It's amazing, but it's pretty hard to keep resenting—even hating—somebody you're praying for. It just kind of works that way.

✿ ***KRESHA: My brothers, the boys at school, and sometimes even the girls at school love to harass me. They hide my things, snap my bra, read my diary out loud. Is it all right that I want to do something to get back at them every time?***

It's all right that you want to, but it's not okay if you do it. Jesus didn't say an eye for an eye (or a boxer-snapping for a bra-snapping). He said to turn the other cheek. That means two things:

1. Don't let the situation become the big deal the teasers hope it will become; this takes away their whole purpose in teasing you in the first place.
2. Turn that cheek so that it's out of the way for the next blow; that means lock your diary and hide it, wear sports bras that aren't so easy to snap—that kind of thing. But don't hide their stuff or snatch their private notes. You're better than that.

Basically, we're looking at four guidelines for every relationship, whether it's between you and your mom, you and your kid brother, you and your best friend, you and you, or you and God.

1. Treat other people, whoever they are, the way you'd like them to treat you.
2. Let other people know that you love and respect them and that you want to be loved and respected too.
3. People are going to make mistakes in their relationships with you, so forgive as often as you have to.
4. Don't hold a grudge or try to get revenge—ever.

Let's use these guidelines to make a Relationship Trouble Spot Checklist.

Just Do It!

Answer these questions by putting check marks in the columns where you think you can answer yes. Leave the rest blank.

Connection Questions

	parents	siblings	friends	boys	elders	myself	God
Do you think you're bossy with?	__	__	__	__	__	__	__
Do you think you're a doormat with?	__	__	__	__	__	__	__
Who doesn't listen to you?	__	__	__	__	__	__	__
Who hurts your feelings?	__	__	__	__	__	__	__
Who needs your forgiveness?	__	__	__	__	__	__	__
Who do you want to get back at?	__	__	__	__	__	__	__

See those check marks? Those are your trouble spots. Let's shoot for them! Are you ready?

God: Your Relationship Counselor

Before we start, there's one more important thing. You can't have fun, hassle-free (or almost hassle-free) relationships that help you grow if you don't let God help you. God knows more about people and the way they relate to each other than anybody—Freud, Dr. Laura, or any of that crowd.

The way to get into all that good wisdom is to know Jesus and not only study what he said when he was down here hanging out, but what he shows you as you follow his way in your life. Just in case you aren't convinced, here's some evidence right from the Bible:

[Jesus] will be called Wonderful Counselor. ***(Isaiah 9:6)***

[Nicodemus] came to Jesus. . .and said, "Rabbi, we know you are a teacher who has come from God." ***(John 3:2)***

"I will ask the Father, and he will give you another Counselor to be with you forever—the Spirit of truth." ***(John 14:16–17)***

So how do we know what Jesus is advising us to do as we follow his way? It isn't tough. You start by praying.

Talking to God About It

To help you start a conversation with God about the trouble spots in your relationships, you might fill in the blanks in this prayer and offer it to the Father in the name of the Son. In fact, you might want to offer it every day for a while and change it as your relationships change. And with God's help, they will change!

Dear ______________ (your favorite way of addressing God),

Thanks for somehow getting this book to me so I can work on my friendships. Please help me to see how important it is to get along well with people, especially the ones who are the most important in my life: ____
I have a lot of trouble getting along with ___________________.
Please help me to treat him/her the way I want him/her to treat me, which is ____.

I am shy or nervous around ________________________. Please build my confidence, Lord, so I can be heard.

I'm having trouble forgiving _____________________ for _________________________. Please help me to forgive as many times as I have to. I'm also feeling like I want to get back at _________________________ for _________________________.

Don't let me do it, God! Help me to let go of my grudge. Thanks for being there to hear all this and help me with it. I know you are my most important relationship of all. I love you!

____________________________ *(your name)*

Lily Pad

Describe one morning in an alone-life (don't forget what might be the attractive parts of that!).

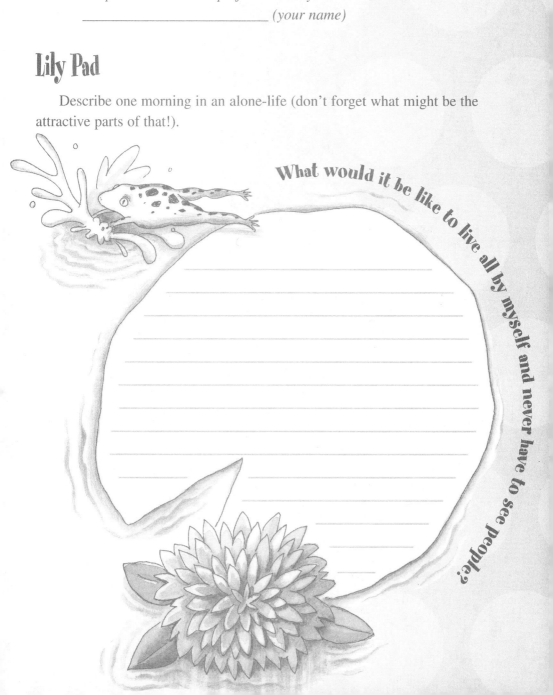

What would it be like to live all by myself and never have to see people?

chapter
2

Raising Good Parents

"Honor your father and your mother, so that you may live long in the land the Lord your God is giving you."
(Exodus 20:12)

Raise my parents? Aren't *they* supposed to be raising *me?*

Of course, your parents are doing *most* of the raising, but you do need to consider that probably nobody sat them down and "taught" them how to be parents. They may have gone to a child-care class to learn how to give you a bath, but mostly they just watched their own parents raising *them*—also without a user's manual—and applied what they picked up to you. The problem is that your parents learned all that before they knew you, and while a lot of the same principles apply to every kid, each person is unique and comes with his or her own set of instructions.

Unfortunately, that set of instructions isn't written out on paper, and besides, what father would ever read it anyway? Dads never read the directions! But you do have a set of instructions built into you, and now that you're old enough, you can start helping your parents know what those instructions are. Yes, the relationship you have with them is mostly determined by *them,* but you have a lot to do with it, and now's the time to start.

Check Yourself Out

Let's take a look at where you are with your parents right now. None of these answers is right or wrong, good or bad, so be honest. Wherever you are, that's just where you are.

Choose the answer under each statement that best fits you:

1. **If my parents weren't my parents and I met them someplace, I would**
   A. like them and wish they were my parents.
   B. ignore them; I mean, they're parents!
   C. really be annoyed by them.

2. **When my parents ask/tell me to do something I don't want to do I**
   A. do it even if I'm not thrilled about it.
   B. argue and complain—and then do it anyway.
   C. just flat-out don't do it.

3. When I have a problem I

A. go to my parents with it no matter what it is.

B. go to my parents with it if it is something my friends can't help me with or if I'm not afraid of what my parents will say.

C. hardly ever go to my parents; they just don't get anything.

4. The difference between the way I act at home and the way I act other places is

A. I'm more comfortable at home than I am with other people unless we're good friends, and then there's no difference.

B. I'm more comfortable and can be myself more with my friends than at home most of the time.

C. I'm totally different; at home I'm basically pretty evil, but I'm nicer with my friends.

5. My personal style and tastes—things like hairdos, clothes, and music—is

A. pretty much the way my parents like it; we don't argue about that stuff.

B. different in some ways than what my parents like; they don't always approve of my choices.

C. the cause of a lot of fights in our house!

6. When I'm at home I

A. spend time wherever the rest of the family is.

B. spend some time with the family and some time by myself.

C. spend almost all my time by myself.

7. When it comes to decisions

A. my parents make most of them, and I'm okay with that.

B. I'd like to make more of my own.

C. I fight hard when my parents try to make any decisions for me.

8. My parents protect me

A. and I like that.

B. too much sometimes; I'd like to be more independent.

C. way too much; they smother me.

9. My parents listen to me

A. always.

B. sometimes.

C. hardly ever.

10. My parents criticize me

A. only when it's for my own good.

B. about a lot of things, and it makes me resentful.

C. about everything—and it makes me want to rip down the wallpaper or something.

11. I please my parents

A. most of the time (but nobody's perfect!)

B. some of the time, but there are still things about me that make them crazy.

C. none of the time; whatever I do never seems to be enough.

12. My parents want me to grow up

A. someday.

B. but they're not really letting me a lot of the time.

C. the sooner the better so I'm out of their hair!

Now go back and count up all the A's, B's, and C's you circled and write your totals in the spaces provided: A ____ B ____ C ____

If you had more A's than you did other letters, things are pretty peaceful at your house, right? Maybe your parents are still very much in charge, and you like it that way. Or maybe they're starting to give you more freedom, and it's working out. You're content with the way things are—so enjoy it! Things may change and get a little rough in the future, or you and your folks may breeze through the whole process. This chapter will help make breezing a bigger possibility, especially if you pay extra attention on the areas where you did have B's and C's.

If you had more B's than you did other letters, things might be a little rocky from time to time between you and your parents. Maybe you're wanting to grow up faster than they're willing to let you. Or perhaps you find yourself resenting things about them that never bothered you before, and you don't even know why. That isn't bad. It's just a sign that you're beginning to become independent, and that's a natural part of growing up. Your becoming independent doesn't have to be an uncomfortable thing for you or your parents. This chapter will help ease the way, especially in the areas you didn't mark as A's.

If you had more C's than you did other letters, chances are your parents and you are in an ongoing battle, and nobody's winning. The fact that it's happening doesn't mean there's anything wrong with you. It means you and your parents have very different views about how you ought to be growing up. The first thing to remember if you fall into this category is that your parents are in charge of you, and you really need to respect that. The second thing to remember is that it is possible for you to work with them so that the rest of your childhood and adolescence doesn't feel like you're in some kind of medieval torture chamber. This chapter is definitely for you.

What's Going on with This Parent Stuff?

If you flip back through your family photos to when you were six and under, you will probably see pictures of you hugging on your parents like they were the Backstreet Boys or following your mom around in her high heels so you could be like her, or looking adoringly up at your dad while you two "danced" with you standing on his feet. When you were little, your parents were the center of your universe, and that was just the way you liked it.

Maybe you still think your parents are the neatest people on the planet, and that's wonderful. You probably also think some other people are just as cool, and you wouldn't want to be without them either—like your best friend, your soccer coach, your favorite aunt, or perhaps—if you're unique!—your older sister.

But at times you may question, at least in your head, your parents' wisdom about things. Maybe their ideas about music, clothes, even who should be president, aren't just like yours anymore. Maybe that's causing some resentment and possibly some arguments. And maybe because of that you're wanting to spend more and more time out of the house with your friends, doing things that don't constantly shout "I'm a member of the Smith family!"

Whether you're at that point or just beginning to find out that it's sometimes fun to be separate from your family, it's all a part of the process that God has in mind for us when he makes us.

HOW IS THIS A God Thing?

God causes you to want to drift away from the old secure life so that gradually the circle of important people in your life will grow bigger and bigger. Try this:

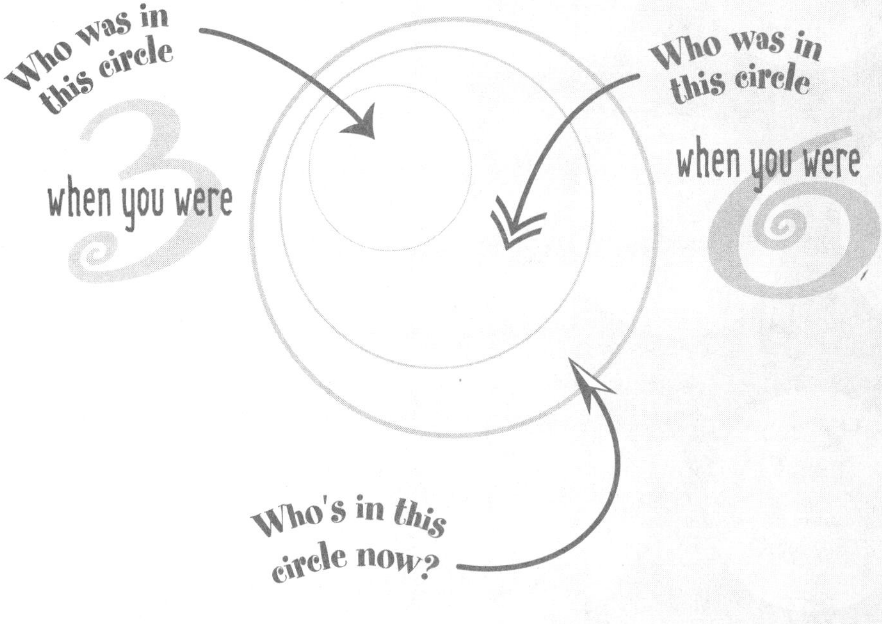
Who was in this circle
when you were
3
Who was in this circle
when you were
6
Who's in this circle now?

It happens that way because of what God said right at the beginning, as recorded in Genesis. He said to Adam, "A man will leave his father and mother and be united to his wife" (Genesis 2:24). The wife, obviously, has to do the same thing. The circle of relationships getting bigger and bigger is preparation for that "leaving," whether you actually get married or not. Growing up and becoming independent involves separating from the family some and identifying with other people. You should be allowed to do that naturally.

Sometimes, though, problems erupt. No kidding! Maybe some of these things are already happening to you or may happen in the future:

- Your parents think you're growing up too fast. They're afraid if they give you too much freedom you'll make a lot of mistakes.
- You're wanting to dress and talk and act differently than you used to, just to be different from your parents.
- Your parents get their feelings hurt every time you want to do something with your friends instead of being with them.
- You don't listen to your parents as much as you used to, because you think you can do things for yourself. You especially don't want to hear about what it was like when your mom was a kid!
- Your parents still want you to hang out with them in the evenings watching TV or whatever, but you want to spend some time in your room by yourself.

So Do I Put a Bag Over My Head and Wait 'Til I Turn Eighteen?

Hardly! There really are some things you can do—even if you're only eight or nine—to smooth out the conflicts you're having or pave the way for smoothing out those that might pop up in the future. After all, relationships always work both ways—they're always the responsibility of both people involved.

Below is a list of things to think about in terms of you and your parents. Put a check next to any of those you think might help you right now. Some you may already be doing; you can leave those blank. Some just might not be a problem for you; leave those blank too. Let's just focus on the ones that really seem to be shouting to you, "Check me! Check me!"

___ 1. Your parents have to be your parents. They have certain responsibilities. They have to make sure you're safe. They have to try to teach you not to become a shoplifter or some other type of juvenile offender. They have to show you decent manners so you don't make an idiot out of yourself in public. They have to give you limits so you don't get into things you aren't ready for. All of that means they have to make decisions about you that you might not be so crazy about. Keep this in mind when you're getting ready to whine about some rule they've made. Your parents have to do the *right* thing, not necessarily the thing that is going to make you happy right this minute. Have they ever said to you, "You'll thank me for this someday"? Chances are, you will!

___ 2. If you think kids whose parents let them do anything they want have better relationships with their parents, you're wrong. Think about this: if your parents didn't set any limits for you—if they said sure, go ride your bike on the freeway—you'd think they didn't care about you. Parents do what they do because they love you.

___ 3. If after thinking about all that, you still think some limit your parents have set is unreasonable for you—like still having to go to bed at 8:00 or still having your mom pick out your clothes every morning or still not being allowed to stay alone in the house for an hour even though you're eleven—you may be able to change your mom or dad's mind if you present your case calmly and in as mature a way as you can. Let's look at an example:

Immature: "Mom, it's *so* stupid that you won't let me stay here by myself for an hour while you go run errands. For Pete's sake, I'm eleven years old. What do you think I'm going to do, stick my finger in a socket or put the cat in the dryer or something if you aren't here to watch me every second? You treat me like a baby!"

Probable Response from Mom: "Yes, I do treat you like a baby, because right now you sound like one. I don't like your disrespectful attitude, young lady. Now get in the car."

Mature: "Mom, when you go run errands tomorrow, do you think I could stay here by myself? I'm thinking that the way I do my homework and chores without being told proves that you can trust me not to get into trouble when I'm alone for an hour. You'll have your cell phone with you, so I could call you if there was a problem. I'd really like to stay here and read."

Probable Response from Mom: "You could have a point. Let me talk it over with your dad."

___ 4. Give your parents a chance to understand the problems you might be going through. They were, after all, your age once, and experience counts for a lot. Maybe your mom didn't argue with her friends over Beanie Babies, but she probably argued with them over Strawberry Shortcake and Her Friends. Maybe your dad was never a girl—well certainly he wasn't!—but he was a boy, so he knows about boys and what absurd little creeps they can be at your age. Fashions change, colors change, music changes—but emotions have been the same since Adam and Eve's kids were growing up. Don't just assume that your parents don't understand you. At least give it a shot.

___ 5. Start getting to know your parents as people rather than as just the mom and dad who give you a roof over your head and drive you all over the place and give you money for the things you need every time you stick out your hand. Look at pictures of them before they had you. What kinds of things were they doing? What do they do now when they're not doing something for you (which is most of the time, by the way!)? Ask them some questions about themselves, like, "Dad, how come you became a doctor?" or "Mom, if you could take a whole year and do whatever you wanted to do, what would you do?" You're going to find that you like your parents as much as you love them, and it's much easier to get along with people you really like. It doesn't take a rocket scientist to figure that out! When you show an interest in them, as opposed to just in yourself, you are showing maturity. Your parents are then just naturally going to start letting you make some simple decisions on your own.

___ 6. Don't expect your parents to read your mind. Tell them—in a mature way—what you want, what you need, how you'd like to see things change. You may take them completely by surprise. On the other hand, they may tell you to dream on, but at least you've tried. Try again when some time has gone by.

___ 7. Pray that your parents will be given guidance by God. One way to do that is simply to say, "God, please make a bridge over that big gap between what I need and what my parents are doing." Do it every day, every time you think about it. God listens and cares and acts.

Just Do It

Pick one of these activities that you think would help your relationship with your parents—or that you think would be fun! Then just do it!

- Write down one interest that you and your dad share and one that you and your mom share.

Mom and I both like to ______________________________

Dad and I both like to ______________________________

Then fill your parents in on your discovery and share your common interest soon.

Examples:

Mom and I both like to:

○ bake cookies
○ see Disney movies and cry
○ go fishing
○ tear pictures out of magazines and put them in scrapbooks

Dad and I both like to:

- ☐ swim.
- ☐ read books like *The Chronicles of Narnia.*
- ☐ take long walks without having to talk.
- ☐ watch old movies and make fun of the acting.

- Put together a fun booklet entitled "Things I Wish My Parents Knew." Use photos, pictures from magazines, your own drawings, stickers—the possibilities are endless. Include the small things that would make *your* life more enjoyable, like "I wish my parents knew that I like to read for at least fifteen minutes in bed before I turn out my light" or "I only like to have my door closed because I like to daydream, not because I'm trying to shut them out." Avoid making it sound like you're criticizing your folks, like "I wish my parents knew that it really annoys me when they try to sing along with the songs I like on the radio," or "My dad dresses like a nerd, and it embarrasses me." Share your booklet with your parents. Be sure to include "I wish my parents knew just how much I love them."
- Write a letter to your parents—one you will never give them—in which you tell them all the things you wish they would do differently. It doesn't matter whether they're reasonable things or not; this is your chance to vent. Get it all out. Read it over. Then tear it into tiny pieces and throw it away. You'll be surprised how just "talking about it" will make you feel better. You'll probably decide that some of the stuff you stewed about isn't worth worrying about anymore. You may get up the courage to present one or two possible changes to your mom and dad. Or you may feel lighter because you got it out.

What If None of That Works? What If My Parent Problems Are Bigger Than That?

Sometimes the conflicts that burst out between growing girls and their parents aren't just the result of the normal move toward independence. Then what do you do?

Girlz WANT TO KNOW

✿ ***SUZY: Whenever my mother gets mad at me, she gives me the silent treatment. Sometimes she won't talk to me for a whole day, and I get so nervous I end up crying in my room. How can I get her to stop doing that?***

You're right to want your mother to stop doing that, because "the silent treatment" doesn't give either of you a chance to work things through together. Have you told your mom that it hurts you when she does that? Have you talked to your dad about it? It's really important that your mother know what it does to you when she shuts you out, so if you have to, write her a letter explaining how you feel. You can even try drawing a picture with a note underneath it. It isn't your responsibility to change your mother, but it is your job to let her know how you feel.

✿ ***ZOOEY: My mom is so overprotective. She won't let me walk my friend home three blocks away. She won't let me answer the front door even if she's in the house. She won't even let me get out of her sight in the grocery store—and I'm eleven years old! Help!***

First of all, it sounds like you are the most important thing in the world to your mom. Be thankful for that, because in other ways, it's a pretty good deal. That's why she helps you with your schoolwork, makes sure you have nice clothes to wear, takes care of you when you're sick—and all that other neat stuff you couldn't live without. But it is hard to feel as if you can't make a move without supervision. The way you're feeling is a sign that you're ready for some independence. Unfortunately, the world we live in has gotten scary. Kids do get abducted on the sidewalk, in grocery stores, and even from their own homes. That's probably why your mom wants you in view at all times! The trick is to strike a balance. Ask yourself some questions and act on them if you need to. Have you explained to your mom—calmly, without whining—how you feel? Have you suggested that maybe she watch you while you walk the three blocks to your friend's house? Have you figured out a signal so that if you were three aisles away in a store, you could give the signal and your mom would know you were in trouble and come running? (This would be like a whistle or something; in our family we make a honking noise!) Have you made a list of the things you would really like to do on your own? Do that and choose the one that seems the safest, like being allowed to answer the front door, and address that with your mom first, suggesting safeguards, such as, "I'll look out the window, and if it's somebody I don't know, I'll yell for you instead of opening the door." When that issue is successfully taken care of, move to the next simplest one on your list. Never push too hard though. Wait a month or two on the ones your mother balks about and try it again.

✿ ***RENI: Whatever I do is never quite good enough for my parents. If I make all A's and one B, my dad wants to know why I got the B and grounds me from TV until I bring it up. If I clean my room, my mom will tell me she still sees dust. Sometimes I feel like a loser. What am I supposed to do?***

You definitely aren't a loser. But it is hard for anybody to deal with constant criticism and the it's-not-quite-good-enough approach without feeling a sense of failure. After a while you might even wonder what's the point and stop trying. Before you get there, consider a few things.

1. Your parents do what they're doing probably because they have high expectations of you. They see you as a capable person, and they want you to live up to your potential. You'll grow up having high expectations of yourself, and that isn't always bad. It'll help you strive to do your best.
2. But no one can shine *all* the time. We all make mistakes. We all have low days. We all have different ideas of what our best is. Keep that in mind at those times when you're feeling as if maybe you aren't good enough. It isn't an excuse—it's real. If you think you've done your best and they don't, that doesn't make you a loser.
3. However, in order to keep resentment from building up, you need to take some steps.

    - **Tell your parents how you feel**—calmly, without whining (sound familiar?). They may not be aware of how frustrated you are.

- **Ask them to tell you what their standards are for each task you have to perform,** whether it's cleaning your room or making grades in school. Ask them to be specific: does Mom want absolutely no dust anywhere, all dust balls out from under the bed, not a speck on a window, socks lined up in the drawer? Does Dad really expect A's in every subject? Look at their lists and tell them whether you think you can live up to their expectations. Perhaps some items might be open for discussion. Your mom may see that vacuuming, dusting, cleaning the windows, and straightening up your closet may be too much for one Saturday morning and be willing to divide that up over several Saturdays.
- **If you really feel that you can't live up to their expectations, ask for help.** If you can't make an A in math, ask your Dad to get you a tutor. If you get overwhelmed when you try to clean your room, ask your mom to show you how she would approach it.
- **Reward yourself for an effort you genuinely think was your best even if they didn't.** Save up your allowance and buy yourself that book or CD or milkshake you've been craving when you bring home a report card you're proud of. It's not a matter of "I don't care what they think." It's a matter of "I know I did my best." After all, you're the only one who can truly know that.

✿ ***KRESHA: I want to be more like my friends—wear clothes like them and listen to the music they do—but my mother says I don't need to, that I need to just be myself. But what if myself is being like my friends? I'm so confused!***

Your problem is confusing. I bet that just like your mom, you want to be the very self that you really are, only right now you're not sure exactly who that is. Part of finding that out is what we call identifying with peers. That means just what you said—acting like your friends, dressing like them, and even talking like them. It's normal for girls your age to want to do that, and in the process they figure out that, no, I don't really feel comfortable in this kind of pants, but yeah, I really do like this kind of music, and I'd listen to it even if nobody else did. Of course, my telling you that this is normal doesn't change your mother's mind! But there are a couple of things you can do about parents who don't like to hear, "Everybody else is doing it!"

- **Don't say "everybody else is doing it,"** or you're sure to hear, "If everybody else were jumping off a cliff, would you jump too?" Parents have been saying that for centuries! Instead, simply present what you'd like to do or buy as something you would like to do.
- **Be sure that what you're asking for is within your parents' reach.** Can they afford it? Do they have time to make it happen for you? You're old enough to consider those kinds of things.
- **Start with something small.** Choose a change you'd like to make that doesn't cost a lot and isn't too dramatic. Maybe you want to wear your hair down and flowing with a crooked part like the other girls instead of up in that tidy ponytail. Present that possibility to your mom, showing her what it will look like, bringing her into it with you. I know you want to make the choice on your own, but some parents need for you to do that gradually.
- **Never, ever do something behind your parents' backs.** If all the other girls are wearing makeup and your dad says no and can't be persuaded, don't keep yours in your desk at school and sneak it on when you get there. You *will* be found out, and then what kind of trust have you established with your parents? That's what honoring your mother and father really means.

✿ ***LILY: Sometimes I get the urge to do something just to be doing it, just because I know it'll make my parents' eyes pop out. You know, like dye my hair green or put a press-on tattoo on my ankle. Does that mean I'm starting to rebel?***

Rebel? Well, in a sense, yes. You want to make a statement: This is me, and I'm not what you think! That's a mild form of rebellion. The trouble for some girls is that it doesn't stop there. They rebel by drinking, taking drugs, sneaking out with older guys, smoking, refusing to go to church—the outlets are almost never-ending. My advice is:

- When you get those twinges and urges, look at why they're happening. Is there something your parents aren't letting you do that you should talk to them about? There's nothing wrong with asking why a certain rule has been put into place, and a lot of times understanding the reason makes the resentment disappear.
- Some "this is me" statements are okay. Things that really show the true you, like wearing a new color or deciding you'd rather take art classes than play soccer, are a healthy part of finding out who you are. Going ahead with them keeps you from feeling like you have to shock somebody with a change.
- Anything that could be hurtful to you or somebody else or that would completely turn most people off to you isn't a healthy way to express your need to break out. Show up at a store with bright green hair, and the manager is going to watch you like a hawk, certain you're about to shoplift him right out of business. Do any body piercing, and watch the infections and the complications arise. You see how it works?
- If the urge to rebel is so strong you're thinking about it all the time, or finding yourself doing things you know are bad news, or feeling anger you can't control, talk to your parents or another adult you trust. You need some help working that through before it starts working you.

Talking to God About It

You have less power in your relationship with your parents than you do in any of your other relationships right now. That's when you need God the most! God has the power both to help you do your part in getting along with your parents and to help your parents make the changes they may need to make.

There is a beautiful, famous prayer that goes like this:

God, grant me the serenity [peacefulness] to accept the things I cannot change, the courage to change the things I can, and the wisdom to know the difference.

You can pray that prayer for you and your parents this way:

Dear ____________ *(your favorite name for God),*

There are things about my parents that just aren't going to change—things like

____

____

____.

Please help me to accept those things and to honor and respect my parents.

There are other things about my relationship with my parents that I'm having a hard time accepting, things like

____

____

____.

Please help me have the courage to talk to my parents about those things. Help me not to whine or yell or be sarcastic. And most of all, Lord, help me see the difference between things they do that I don't like that just aren't going to change and the things I can do something about. Thanks, God. I sure appreciate it.

Love,

____________________ *(your name)*

Lily Pad

Imagine a perfect afternoon with your mom. Describe what you'd do, what you'd talk about, how it would feel. Go into lots of mother-daughter detail! (You can do this for your dad instead, or even do both. Just draw more pads!)

Imagine a perfect afternoon with your mom . . .

chapter
3

Taming Siblings

A friend loves at all times,
and a brother is born for adversity.
(Proverbs 17:17)

Then how come God gave us brothers and sisters in the first place?

It seems that ever since Cain killed his brother Abel (Genesis 4:2–8), brothers and sisters have been going at it, and for the same reasons.

The Lord looked with favor on Abel and his offering, but on Cain and his offering he did not look with favor. So Cain was very angry, and his face was downcast. (Genesis 4:4–5)

Present day translation: Your little sister gets straight A's, and your parents turn somersaults. You get B's, and they want to know why you can't be more like her. Your face is, shall we say, "downcast."

The Lord said to Cain, "Where is your brother Abel?"
"I don't know," he replied. "Am I my brother's keeper?" (Genesis 4:9)

Present day translation: Your mom goes into the laundry room, and when she comes out, your baby brother has scribbled all over the dining room wall. "Why did you let him do that?" she says to you. "It's not my day to watch him," you say.

The Lord said, "You will be a restless wanderer on the earth." Cain said to the LORD, "My punishment is more than I can bear." (Genesis 4:12–13)

Present day translation: Your dad says, "You pinched your sister. You're grounded for a week." You cry (with much gnashing of teeth), "That's not fair! I'll die of boredom!"

Although Cain and Abel had a disastrous relationship, God kept giving people siblings—brothers and sisters. Cain's descendants Jabal and Jubal were brothers. (I bet it was confusing in that house!) Tubal-Cain, their cousin, had a sister named Namaah. And meanwhile, Adam and Eve had another brother for Cain (as if he hadn't abused the first one enough!), and his name was Seth.

Chances are it's the same in your family. Both your parents probably had siblings they fought with over stuff like who got to sit in the front seat and which cartoons they were going to watch on Saturday mornings. But did that stop them from producing siblings for you? Unless you're an only child, no way. No matter how much brothers and sisters argue and tease and torment each other, parents just keep making families they have to referee. What's up with that? Wouldn't life be a lot simpler if the Lord just gave each set of parents one kid and let it go at that?

HOW IS THIS A God Thing?

If I required you to answer how brothers and sisters are a God-thing, you might have a hard time. Maybe just this week alone your sister got on the school bus behind you wearing your new top, your brother scratched your favorite CD using it for a Frisbee, and both of them got to go to McDonald's with your mom while you were being tutored in English by some cranky retired teacher who made you diagram sentences for an hour. That makes it pretty hard to see that God really intended for it to be this way!

But look a little closer. If a bunch of girls at school ganged up on that same sister who wore your new top, what would you do about it? And if that same little brother who Frisbeed your CD out of operation were suddenly diagnosed with leukemia, how would you feel? And if both of them pooled their allowance to buy you cool hair gizzies for your birthday, how would you react?

In spite of all the bickering over who gets to hold the remote and who gets cut more slack by Mom and Dad, the bond between siblings is as deep and fierce as any other you'll have in your lifetime. Loyalty and love were both in that gene pool you all came from, and no matter how furious you may get with your brothers and sisters, you can't deny that you'd stand up for them no matter what, that you'd be devastated if something happened to one of them, that you'd be touched if they did something nice (and out of character!) for you. It's a tight relationship, one other relationships sometimes envy. In Song of Songs 8:1, the Beloved even says to the Lover, "If only you were to me like a brother." Brothers and sisters who have every right to hate each other's guts somehow manage to keep on loving each other. Look at Joseph, son of Jacob, in the Bible. His brothers sold him off into slavery, and he still saved them from starvation years later! In fact, when Jesus was teaching, he used the word *brother* to show people how he wanted them to love one another. He said, "Whoever does the will of my Father in heaven is my brother and sister …" (Matthew 12:50).

Putting kids together in a family is one of the ways God influences your growing up. Here's how it works:

- How your brothers and sisters react to you affects how you see yourself. If you're the oldest and they're always coming to you for help with their homework or to borrow your stuff or just to hang out with you (gag!), you may see yourself as a leader-type. If your brothers and sisters always depend on you to come up with ideas, you may see yourself as creative. If your siblings just don't get where you're coming from half the time, you may see yourself as "different." See how it is?
- The competition among you helps shape what you want. If you've had to share a room with your sisters all your life, and they always seem to get more space than you, one of your greatest desires may be for room—and lots of it. If you try and try but your brother always gets better grades, you may long to be smarter.
- The way you all treat each other partly forms how you see the world. If you have to scrap and fight for everything, it's more than likely a dog-eat-dog world in your eyes. If you share everything—and not at gunpoint only!—the world may look friendlier and more giving to you.

But does God want all the arguing and vying for attention that goes on among brothers and sisters? Did God create sibling rivalry?

Since competing with each other for your parents' attention and approval and involvement in your life is very human, chances are God does allow it, because:

- it helps you learn how to be assertive and how to ask for what you need and want.
- it helps you learn how to fight fair and deal with conflicts out there in the rest of the world.
- it helps you learn how to cooperate, how to work as a team, and how to compromise when you need to.

In fact, those of you who are only children may find it tougher for a while when you go off to college or get your first job and find out that not everybody is as considerate of your space and your feelings as your parents have been. Those with brothers or sisters learned that back in the playpen!

Where Are You with Your Siblings Right Now?

Let's see where you stand on this brother-sister thing. Put a check mark next to every statement below that is true for you. If you're an only child, read through the quiz anyway. It may help you understand what your friends are going through.

☐ 1. I think my siblings get more from my parents than I do.
☐ 2. I have at least one sibling who always tries to be better than me.
☐ 3. I think my parents have favorites among us kids.
☐ 4. When my brother or sister starts liking or doing something I liked or did first, I stop doing it.
☐ 5. When my brother or sister starts doing or liking something new, I start doing it too, because I want to be just like him or her.
☐ 6. I don't even try in a certain area—like grades or sports or beauty or popularity—because that's my sister's or brother's "turf."
☐ 7. My siblings and I fight a lot. Sometimes we even come to blows!
☐ 8. I have a sibling who makes nasty remarks about me—calls me Jabba the Hutt, that kind of thing.
☐ 9. I have a sibling I make nasty remarks about, saying he's such a nerd he should be wearing a pocket protector or making other such comments.
☐ 10. I have a brother or sister who is always stirring up trouble—things like telling me I'm adopted.
☐ 11. I find myself stirring up trouble for my brother or sister, saying stuff like, "Mom bought me ice cream while you were at your piano lesson. Neener-neener."
☐ 12. The way my sibling(s) tease me and joke around with me gets way out of hand. My feelings get hurt.

☐ 13. I can't help teasing my sibling(s) even though I know he or she is going to end up crying any minute

Count up your check marks and put the number here: ____

If you had between nine and thirteen check marks, chances are you and your fellow siblings are like a pack of cats in a room with only one mouse. Maybe you've figured that that's just the way it is with brothers and sisters. Figure again! You're at a place in your life where you can do something to change that. No, you can't trade your siblings in for newer models. But you can change your attitude toward them, how you behave with them, and maybe even influence them to do some changing of their own. Hey, stranger things have happened—and why waste any time being completely miserable with the very people you have the strongest bond with? Read on!

If you had between four and eight check marks, things aren't too obnoxious at your house, but they could use attention in some areas. This chapter can help you zero in on the conflicts that could easily be evaporated and the ones that might take more work but can still be fixed. Yes, some conflict is normal, but you can get rid of the stuff that isn't.

If you had between zero and three check marks, you're either the only kid left living at home, your siblings are infants, or you've really learned how to live together. Congrats! Just in case you need it in the future, read what this chapter has to say, especially in the areas you checked. Relationships are always changing, and they always take work to be their best.

Tell Me Again Why I Should Go to All This Trouble

- Relationships among siblings are bound to be rocky sometimes, considering all the competition that goes on.
- We learn from that rockiness.
- But when the rifts between you and your brothers and sisters get ugly or keep you from making good choices, there are ways to work them out.
- Then you'll be able to get all the good out of that tight, fierce bond God made for you.

So How Do I GET OUT—and STAY OUT—of the Sibling Combat Zone?

Girlz WANT TO KNOW

✿ ***LILY: I'm getting along better with my older brother because he's too busy with his own life to pick on me anymore. But my younger brother still makes rude comments about me every chance he gets. He'll say stuff like, "When did we get a new dog? Oh, it's Lily." How can I get him to knock it off?***

Have you considered duct tape? No, seriously, there are a couple of different approaches you could take with a rude sibling:

1. You could make a vow not to respond to any of his comments no matter how rude they are. It would take enormous will power, and your brother's verbal attacks might get worse for a while in an attempt to get to you (something that obviously gives him great pleasure). But eventually—at least before you graduate and move out—he'll give up and stop. If he's not getting what he wants—a reaction from you—why do it?
2. You could ask your parents for help, explaining to them how much it hurts you when he says mean things to you. They may give you the above advice, or they may pay more attention when your brother starts flipping rude remarks your way. Either way, you have nothing to lose.

Whichever action you decide to take, remember this:

- Do not let what your brother says about you determine who you think you are. Just because he says you resemble something out of Veggie Tales doesn't mean you actually do.
- Do not fight fire with fire, hurling negative comments back at him whenever he hurls them at you first. You'll feel lousy about yourself for one thing, and, besides, that's only going to give him an excuse to keep teasing you and trying to outdo you insult for insult.

- In fact, you might try complimenting your brother every time you see a chance. Such opportunities might be few and far between at first, but if you really look hard, you'll find something nice you can say about the little urchin. If you're sincere, it may set him back a rude retort or two. Try it if you have the stomach for it.

✿ ***RENI: I'm an only child. Does that mean I'm going to turn out to be selfish?***

Not at all! You probably feel well taken care of and loved, so enjoy that. You can love having your parents' spotlight all to yourself without becoming self-centered. Just make sure you participate in group activities like teams and camps and clubs. If you have cousins who are kids, ask if you can spend time with them. Invite friends over to your house to spend the night or maybe even see if your parents will let one of them go on a short family trip with you. Just as God allows siblings—and rivalry—God also allows solo kids like you. Enjoy your happy family of three.

✿ ***SUZY: My older sister and my mother are very close. They both like to go clothes shopping and do each other's nails and hair and things like that. They can talk for hours without running out of things to say. But I'm not interested in any of the stuff they like. I'd rather be playing soccer or doing gymnastics. And when I'm with them, I can't think of anything to say. Is it possible for a mom to love one daughter more than the other?***

Your mother doesn't love your sister more than she loves you, I'll guarantee you that. But she loves the two of you in different ways because you're obviously two very different people. It sounds like you would like to be closer to your mom than you are, just as your sister is, and that can happen. Here are a few things you can try:

- Tell your mom you would like to spend some time alone with her. She might not even realize you want that, especially if you tend to be very quiet.
- Have a plan for something you'd like to do with your mom. Maybe ask if she can come to one of your soccer games and afterward go with you

to Baskin Robbins or Taco Bell so you can tell her about your experience in the game.

- Show an interest in what your mom and sister are doing, even if it's not your thing. We can always learn something new; we should never close ourselves off from possibilities.

As you work on this, remember these things:

- Your mom doesn't love your sister more than you. They just have a different relationship.
- Try not to take out your feelings on your sister; it's not her fault she and your mom share similar tastes.
- Always let the people you love know how you feel.

✿ ***ZOOEY: My older brother is the biggest troublemaker. Whenever things are going along fine, he stirs something up. For example, the other day I was doing my math homework, and I was finally understanding it, and I knew I was going to get a good grade on the quiz the next day—finally. Then he comes along and grabs my last quiz, which I got a D on, out of my binder and waves it at my mom and says, "Hey, Mom, did you see this?" She hadn't seen it because I hadn't shown it to her, so I got in trouble. Can't I just bop him over the head, just once?***

Nah. Physical punishment won't stop him. Besides, there are better ways. First, remember that the way your brother is acting is part of sibling rivalry. He's trying to get your mom's attention—show her he's one up on you. As an added bonus, if she gets on your case, as she did this time, that makes him feel superior, at least for a couple of minutes. That isn't right, but it's the reason.

So don't give your brother a reason to pull this stuff on you. Pay him a sincere compliment whenever you can think of one. Don't react to his troublemaking with shrieks and fits; try to ignore him. And—now this one's a stretch, but consider it—you might want to make him your ally. You get a D on a quiz? Go to him and say, "Do you think I should tell Mom? I'm doing better in math now." Okay, so maybe he's not ready for that yet, but keep it in mind. And be patient—he will grow up.

Oh, and if your brother is really being cruel, talk to your parents about it when he isn't around. Without whining, tell them how much it hurts you that he looks for ways to make trouble for you. They love you, and they don't want you to be unhappy.

✿ ***KRESHA: I have two younger brothers, and the three of us fight like there is a war going on. We don't just argue. We scratch and bite and pull hair. I try not to get into that with them, but I have to defend myself! If my mom knew we were beating each other up, she'd be so mad. I don't know what to do, and someday somebody's really going to get hurt.***

A little wrestling around among brothers and sisters is normal, but what you're describing sounds like the World Wrestling Federation, and that isn't normal! Nothing is ever solved through physical violence. It's just a way for people to express anger and frustration. Here's what you can try before somebody puts an eye out:

- Don't take it on yourself to stop this pattern of fighting. Your mom needs to know. She may get mad, but so what? Would you rather see your mom upset for five minutes or see one of your brothers knock your front teeth out? She needs to know so she can deal with the two of them.
- As soon as your brothers start doubling their fists and getting that look in their eyes, get away from them, as far away as you can, even if it means locking yourself in the bathroom until they calm down. If you don't give them somebody to punch, the sizzle will go out of them.
- Look at the kinds of things you're fighting over and see what we've said in this chapter that might help you avoid the arguments or end them before the bloodshed starts.
- Don't listen to people who say they'll grow out of it. It needs to be nipped before it has any more time to grow. Violence, once it's learned, is a hard habit to break.

Let's try to sum up what we've said about the sibling combat zone. Next to each statement below you might want to write how what you have learned can help you with a conflict with which you and your brothers and sisters are dealing with.

Battle Plan A: Try not to respond to sibling behavior that is designed to get to you.

I will ignore ______________ when he/she ______________________ to annoy me.

Battle Plan B: Involve your parents, not by tattling, but by sharing with them how what your sister or brother is doing is affecting you.

I will talk to Mom/Dad about ______________________ and how he/she is____.

Battle Plan C: Don't lower yourself to the same tactics your brother or sister is using. That will just keep things stirred up and will make you feel crummy about yourself.

I'm going to stop ____________________ when _________________ starts in with his/her ____________________________________.

Battle Plan D: Try to be positive. Compliment your brother or sister even if he/she never does that for you. Show an interest in him/her. Ward off conflicts with a better plan.

Today I'm going to tell _______________________________ that I like ________________________ about him/her. I might even ask him/her about ______________________. Maybe I'll really go all out and invite him/her to ______________________________________.

Make Friends–with MY BROTHER?

"You're kidding, right? You expect me to treat my sister like a *friend?* Actually hang out with her?"

Well, yeah. Your sister or brother is the offspring of your parents just like you, and so she or he has just as good a chance of being a cool person as you do. Why miss out? If you have to live together, why not at least attempt to be friends?

"But I'm disgusting to him!"

"She makes fun of everything I do!"

"I basically think he's a geek."

"I don't *want* to hang around with somebody who imitates my every move."

Really? But doesn't Jesus himself say that if we only love the people who are easy to be with, we're not much better than your basic shoplifter or hub-cap stealer, who also loves the people he gets along with? Jesus says love those who "hate" you—who "persecute" you. I think we can translate that into, "Love those in your house who pick on you, tease you, hold their noses when you walk into the room, wear high socks with shorts in public, and follow you around like a puppy." Now that's true Christianity!

This doesn't mean you have to become best friends and go everywhere together. It does mean:

- Look for the best in your brothers and sisters; overlook their obvious flaws for a minute and notice what's cool, nice, cute, fun, fascinating in them. Keep looking—you'll find something!
- Tell your siblings what you discovered.
- Treat your siblings the way you'd like them to treat you whether they do the same or not.
- Forgive your siblings when they hurt your feelings, take your stuff, embarrass you, or get you in trouble. Confront it. Deal with it. Then let it go. No grudges. No revenge. It's over, so move on.

Treat your brothers and sisters the way you treat your friends, and you'll be amazed at how much more peaceful things can be. And if you can do all that, you might want to go one step further.

Just Do It

Ready for the ultimate test? Plan something at least semi-special for you and one of your fellow siblings—preferably one you don't usually get along with or whom you ignore most of the time. Then see if you can pull this off:

1. Think of one thing you and that brother or sister have in common. Do you like the same baseball team? Do you compete for grades because you both like to be at the head of your class? Would each of you kill

for the last blob of cookie dough in the bowl? You may have to dig deep, but you'll come up with something.

2. Now think of a way you could share that common ground. Next time that team plays on TV, whip up some nachos and invite him/her to watch with you—and let him/her hold the remote control for channel flipping during commercials. Treat him/her to a cheap shopping spree at the Dollar Store for making the same or better grades than you did last report card. Invite him/her to make cookie dough with you and split a portion of the dough fifty-fifty and eat it together. It doesn't have to be a big deal—just something to show your sibling that you realize he/she is a person not so totally different from you.
3. Treat your sibling as someone special every once in a while and see what happens. A friendship may blossom. If not, what have you lost?

Talking to God About It

You can do all of the above and still find your little sister going through your diary or continue to endure your big brother's sarcastic remarks about your baby fat. There's only one way you can come out of it without an emotional scratch, and that's to go to the heavenly Father who can, in his mysterious way, solve all problems in ways we hadn't dreamed of.

So make a list of the problems you have with your siblings. Take your list to some private place where no siblings can possibly hide and make fun of you, and name them all off to God. Then fold your paper between your hands, bow your head, and just be quiet for a little while. You might not hear anything, but you can bet God is working in you. Do that as often as you can, especially when things get really difficult with your siblings. God listens. God cares. God acts.

Amen!

Lily Pad

Write out a conversation you would love to have with your brother or sister

chapter 4

The Care and Keeping of Friends

A friend loves at all times.
(Proverbs 17:17)

Finally, we get to the kind of relationship that's probably at the top of your list right now: your friends. Can you even imagine a world without girlfriends?

> Who would you sit with at lunch?
> Who would you call when you found out you had to have braces?
> Who would you tell when your mom said you could have your ears pierced?
> Who would sit up and talk with you half the night about . . . everything?

No matter how close you are to your parents or your brothers and sisters or even to the lady next door, it would be pretty lonely growing up without your best same-age buds.

That isn't an accident—it's meant to be that way at this point in your life.

Why Is It All About Friends Right Now?

If you think back a few years, you may remember a time when you had friends, but you would still rather be with your mom or your dad or your grandmother than anybody else. Things have changed though, right? Now the idea of spending the night with a friend, of sitting next to your best friend on the bus on a field trip, of having your friends over for your birthday—those things may occupy more of your thoughts than just about anything else.

That doesn't mean you don't love your family anymore! It just means you're at that place in your life when, like just about everything else, you're changing.

You're having experiences outside your safe family circle.

You're learning what it takes to have a successful relationship with a person you pick out.

You're figuring out how to resolve conflicts with people who don't *have* to love you.

You're forming ideas and opinions of your own.

You're looking for people who are facing the same kinds of problems you are who will understand just exactly what you're going through.

You're doing the maturing thing—and the friendships you're forming right now are really, really important to that process. While you're throwing pillows at each other at sleepovers and passing notes during the geography lesson, you are actually making a shift from being completely dependent on your parents to being independent, able to take total care of yourself. That shift isn't going to be complete for a while, but having friends prepares you for your future as an adult, when you'll have more dealings with people outside your family than you do with people inside it. Even as we speak, your friends are helping you make an important transition, and you're helping them. No wonder it's such a big deal.

Besides that, there are other benefits that make friendships as important to you right now as food, water, and a decent pair of jeans:

- Friendship is good for your health—seriously. Scientific evidence proves that when you're with your friends and things are going well your blood pressure drops, your stomach acids are reduced, and your heart rate even slows down to a more relaxed pace.
- Friendship makes you feel good about you. When you have friends, you're reminded that you matter, that you're at least a little bit special.
- Friendship makes you feel alive, because you and your friend are always sharing new discoveries.
- Friendship makes you feel secure, because close friends know they're equal to each other and they're comfortable with each other.

Who *doesn't* want to feel healthy, special, alive, and secure? But friendship takes work, and it can have problems. Not to worry though, because like anything else that's really worth it, there are "instructions" for making, being, and keeping friends. They come straight from God.

Friendship Basics—HOW IS THIS A God-Thing?

First off, the Bible is loaded with examples of legendary friendships.

- **David and Jonathan.** Jonathan loved David as much as he loved himself.
- **Job and his three buddies, Eliphaz, Bildad, and Zophar.** They dropped everything and went to Job to give sympathy and comfort when he was having big-time problems.

- **Ruth and Naomi.** Ruth was willing to leave everything she'd ever known just to be with Naomi, who, as you may know, was her mother-in-law.
- **Daniel and his three sidekicks, Shadrach, Meshach, and Abednego.** He got them good jobs, and they were loyal to him through everything.
- **Jesus and his disciples.** They ate, lived, and traveled together for about three years.
- **Paul and his crew, Luke, Mark, Timothy, Priscilla, Aquila**—the list goes on. With all Paul had to do, he still kept track of them, advising them, getting help from them—everything that friends do.

Second, God gives bits and pieces of "advice to the friendly" throughout the Scriptures—things like:

A despairing man should have the devotion of his friends. ***(Job 6:14)***

Do not forsake your friend. ***(Proverbs 27:10)***

A man of many companions may come to ruin, but there is a friend who sticks closer than a brother. ***(Proverbs 18:24)***

These passages would indicate that friendship has been a big thing with people since creation. Just to make sure we know how important it is though, God spells it out in detail in Ecclesiastes:

Two are better than one,
because they have a good return for their work:
If one falls down,
his friend can help him up.
But pity the man who falls
and has no one to help him up!
Also, if two lie down together, they will keep warm.
But how can one keep warm alone?
Though one may be overpowered,
two can defend themselves.
A cord of three strands is not quickly broken.

(Ecclesiastes 4:9–12)

It doesn't get any plainer than that!

Girlz WANT TO KNOW

So How Do You Make Friends?

✿ ***RENI: People talk about how making friends takes work, but it isn't that hard for me. Am I doing something wrong?***

No way! Be grateful that you're the kind of person who is naturally outgoing and friendly and just seems to attract people. Of course, you don't want to take that for granted and assume you can treat your friends however you please because you figure there are more where they came from! More on that later.

✿ ***SUZY: I'm so shy that it's really hard for me to make friends. I'm much more comfortable at home, but I get really lonely sometimes.***

Of course you get lonely, because as we've already seen, girls your age are meant to have friends. But you aren't alone in your shyness. One study shows that about 84 million Americans consider themselves to be shy. It's really natural for some girls, like you, to feel safer in their familiar surroundings than they do at school or at dance class or on the softball field. So pray for some courage, and then ask someone you like to come to that place where you feel safe—your house. Have a focus, like a movie you two could watch together, or a baking project for both of you to do, or a board game to play while you share a bowl of popcorn. Let it be something you're good at or really enjoy, that you've been wishing you could do with somebody. Then, before she comes over, think about how the visit would go if you weren't shy. Sometimes daydreaming with God about a situation makes it less scary to face once it's really happening. Finally, when your new friend arrives, try to concentrate on her—what she likes to do, what would make her feel comfortable. When you take your mind off of yourself, you

automatically become less self-conscious. Once you get comfortable with your new friend, you'll be able to venture out and do more things away from home. Take it slowly, and don't forget to stay close to God!

✿ ***ZOOEY: There are a lot of girls I'd like to be friends with, but I don't tell them that because I wonder why they'd want to be friends with me. I'm overweight, I don't make good grades, and I'm not athletic. Wouldn't they rather be friends with somebody else?***

Whoa, girlfriend! Sounds like we need to work on your self-esteem, (or what we call God-esteem), and we will in chapter 6. Meanwhile, keep a few things in mind:

- Try not to assume that you're going to be rejected. You might have convinced yourself that if you tell someone you want to be friends and she turns you down, you'll feel worse than if you had just kept quiet about it. Don't let that fear hold you back. That isn't God talking at all.
- Most of the time you're the only one who notices all those things you think will keep you from making friends—your weight, your grades, your lack of athletic ability. If we use your class at school as an example, most of the girls there are focusing on themselves too. I bet that girl you'd like to get to know has a whole collection of her own stuff she's stewing about, so she hasn't had time to notice yours! The last thing you want to do when you *do* approach this girl is bring up what you think are your own shortcomings, because chances are she never even thought about them.
- We'll talk more about this later, but for now, make a list of your best qualities, everything you can think of, from the way you laugh so easily to how well you draw. If you have trouble making a list of more than a few things, get God in on it with you. Pray that God will bring those things to mind. Then study that list. Wouldn't you like to be friends with the girl you've just described? Then why wouldn't somebody else?
- You don't have to march right up to that girl you admire and say, "Hi. Wanna be best friends?" Instead, ask her a few questions about herself when you end up standing in line next to her at the water fountain.

When you pass her on the way to the pencil sharpener, tell her you like her shirt or her new backpack. When you see her in the cafeteria, tell her about something neat that just happened to you. Allow a friendship to grow naturally, and it will.

- Be sure you haven't set your sights on a friendship just because the girl is the most popular chick in the class. Make certain you want to be her friend because you really like the person she is. A friendship should never be a way to make you feel important. Besides, often those kinds of "friends" are the very ones who will reject people.

✿ ***KRESHA: I'm the new kid in my class, and it's so hard to make friends. It's like there are only so many spaces for friends, and those are already filled up. What can I do?***

There is always room for one more friend—the spaces are never "filled up." Keep that in mind during these lonely first weeks, because it does take time to form the close relationships we want so much. You have two jobs right now. One is to meet people, and the other is to get acquainted with the ones you "click" with. That's when two people realize they have things in common, that it's easy for them to talk to each other, that they'd like to spend more time together. Nobody knows why some people click and others don't—I'm thinking it's a God-thing. But the point is, we all have people we will click with. It's just a matter of finding them and being open to them when they show up. For how to make friends, read the answers to Suzy and Reni and Zooey's questions. Here are a few suggestions for how to meet new people:

- Ask your teacher(s) if there are any other "new girls" in your class(es). Sometimes misery loves company!
- Join in some after-school activities, maybe a sports team, church group, or scout troop. When you're involved in activities with people, you can't help meeting them and getting to know them. Just be sure the things you participate in are things you really enjoy, because that's where you'll meet the most people who like to do the things you do.
- Ask your teacher if you can bring in something to share with the class, something that will get them asking questions about you. Does your

mom or dad have an interesting job they could talk to the class about? Do you have a cool pet? A collection? A hobby? Or maybe the teacher will let you bring in a batch of cookies to share with the class as a thank you for welcoming you to the class. The people who come up to thank you may be the ones you'll want for friends.

- Every time you interact with somebody you haven't actually met yet, introduce yourself and say hi—somebody who turns around to pass papers back to you, the kid who always gets to school early like you do, the girl whose locker or cubby hole is next to yours. Some people might blow you off, but others will introduce themselves and be friendly. They're the ones who will make the effort worth it.

✿ ***LILY: Some girls are so outgoing they seem to have a thousand friends. Everybody knows them, and they get along with every person on the planet. I'm not like that. I have four close friends, and that makes me happy. Should I try to change and be more popular?***

Absolutely not! There's nothing wrong with being popular, having a lot of friends, being at the center of everything all the time. First, we couldn't all do that, because there wouldn't be room at the center. Second, that isn't the only place that makes a person special. You are you, and as long as you're happy and comfortable in your small circle of friends, that's exactly where you should be. For a minute, pay attention to the phrase "as long as you're happy and comfortable." Use this checklist to be sure you really are happy and comfortable. Check those you would answer yes to:

- ○ Are you afraid that if you try to make more friends you'll be rejected?
- ○ Are there other girls you'd like to become friends with outside your "circle," but you don't want to hurt your present friends' feelings by adding new girls?
- ○ Do you think the people in your small group of friends are the only people you could ever be friends with?
- ○ Do you and your friends spend time gossiping about people who aren't your friends, putting them down or shutting them out?

If you answered yes to any of those questions, think and pray carefully about the ones you checked. They aren't healthy reasons for limiting your number of friendships. But if you didn't answer any with a yes, you probably are happy right where you are. Enjoy!

Once I Have Friends, How Do I Keep Them?

The answer is simple: if you want to *keep* a friend, then *be* a friend. And be a good one.

How? First and foremost, be exactly who you are—no acts, no airs, no fake stuff just to hold onto a friendship. Simply relax and be the unique person God made you to be.

Then make sure you practice the nine things below. Without them, a friendship can't be fun, safe, healthy, or any of the other things you want and need it to be.

✓ CHECK Yourself OUT

Think about your best friend or your closest friend. Write her (or his) name here: ______________

Now pray that God will help you be honest with yourself as you consider your friendship with that person. Put a check in front of each statement that describes you in the friendship.

☐ 1. I'm always honest with my friend no matter what I'm afraid she's going to think of me, no matter how much I want to impress her, no matter what the results might be if I tell the truth. I'm honest with my friend even if I think the truth might hurt her feelings or make her mad. I'm honest even if I don't think she'll understand.

☐ 2. I talk to my friend about the problems we have. When I get mad at her, I don't just keep it inside and get resentful.

☐ 3. I talk to my friend about the good things in our relationship. When she does something nice for me or I just get this flood of liking-her feelings, I tell her.

☐ 4. I listen to my friend when she talks to me. I'm not thinking about what I'm going to say next or butting in with my advice. I let her talk just as much as I talk—and I really listen.

☐ 5. I help my friend when she's upset, and when other people are rude to her, I stand up for her, even if it means they might start in on me! I never talk bad about her behind her back, and I wouldn't even think about backing out on something I told her I'd do for her. She can always count on me.

☐ 6. I share a lot of things with my friend—my free time, my stuff, what I'm thinking. I guess you could say I share myself with her.

☐ 7. My friend can tell me a secret, and I will never breathe a word of it to anybody (unless it's about something that could hurt her, and then I'll tell a grown-up, but not the other kids).

☐ 8. I think of my friend and me as equals—neither one of us is better than the other. I treat her the way I want her to treat me, because we are both God's children and are equal in his eyes. I never laugh at her or put her down. I try to make her see how wonderful she is.

☐ 9. I never take my friend for granted. I don't assume she's always going to be there and then treat her any old way. I'm grateful for our friendship, and I do the best I can to make sure we stay friends.

If you put a check next to all nine statements, you're a great friend. Keep it up. Your friends are blessed to have you.

If you checked between six and eight statements, you're being a good friend. Do study the ones you didn't check, as I'll show you below. After all, friendship is precious, so you have to take good care of it.

If you checked between three and five statements, you're certainly not a "bad friend," but maybe friendship isn't always as good as you want it to be. Now you know some of the reasons, so study the ones you didn't check, as I'll show you below. Pray your way along, and your friendships are going to shape up nicely.

If you checked less than three statements, I bet you're lonely or anxious or often unhappy. Don't beat yourself up. Just study the statements you didn't check, as I'll show you below. Pray a lot for God's help in this. Slowly, things will begin to change. Change really does start with you and God.

Here's the "Be a Friend" course straight from Paul's first letter to the Corinthians, chapter 13. People often think he's talking about love between married people, but he's talking about all love, *especially* love between friends. The things Paul says match up with the checklist above. Imagine that!

Statements 1, 2, and 3: "Love does not delight in evil but rejoices with the truth" (verse 6). Work on being honest no matter what.

Statement 4: "Love is patient, love is kind" (verse 4). Work on communicating—both talking and listening.

Statement 5: Love "always protects, always trusts, always hopes, always perseveres" (verse 7). Work on being loyal.

Statements 6, 7, and 8: Love "does not envy, it does not boast, it is not proud. It is not rude, it is not self-seeking, it is not easily angered, it keeps no record of wrongs" (verses 4–5). Work on sharing and being worthy of your friends' trust.

Statement 9: "Love never fails" (verse 8). Keep working on it!

More Things Girlz WANT TO KNOW

✿ ***LILY: Even my best friend sometimes tells me I can be bossy. I don't know how to stop though. Sometimes it's like I'm the only one who knows what to do, so shouldn't I tell other people?***

Well, Lily, like everything else that is a part of you, or anybody, sometimes it serves you well, and sometimes it doesn't. There are probably times when your being able to see things clearly and take charge is just what everybody needs. Say somebody gets hurt and you're the only one who knows first-aid, or you're doing a group project and everybody else is messing around and you get them back on track so you can get the thing done. But there are other times when compromising would be the far better choice: when it comes to deciding about fun stuff (what to have on the pizza, what to do at the sleepover, how to divide up the teams for volleyball); when it involves matters of taste (what's a good movie, good music, cute clothes); when it really doesn't matter who's right. If you're used to being in charge, it may take time and practice for you to tell the difference and then act that way. It might even take your friends a while to get used to it, and they may still look to you for all the answers. But if you learn to listen to other people's ideas, you're going to discover a whole new world that you were missing while you were trying to control others! It will also take a lot of pressure off of you—you can enjoy yourself more. Just pray each time you come into a situation ripe for your bossiness—"God, do I really need to take over?" The answer will come.

✿ ***SUZY: I have one friend who always seems to do everything better than I do. I know I'm not supposed to be envious or jealous, but I can't help it. Every time she gets an A+ or an award or something, I can hardly congratulate her. Am I an awful person?***

You are not an awful person. You are a human person. That doesn't mean though that you shouldn't work on the competition you seem to have going with your friend. You're obviously unhappy with the way you're feeling, so why not change that? Here are some things you can do:

- Accept that she's getting more recognition for some things right now; that's just the way it is. Gnawing on it like a bone is only going to make you feel worse.
- Think about how happy you would want her to be for you if things were the other way around. In that moment when you get that thought in your head, either go up and congratulate her or write her a note. Be as sincere as you can without gritting your teeth!
- Think about the things you'd like to do well. Do you want to do well because *you* want to do well, or because *she's* doing well? If you want to get the award or the A+ because it would really prove to you that you're doing your best in something that's important to you, go for it. But do it because you want to, not because you want to be better than she is. If you realize you have the wrong motive, make a list of the things you would *really* like to excel in and go after those things. You may rise to the top in something completely different than what she's going after, and then you'll both feel like winners. Just remember through it all though that being the best, the winner, the gold medalist, isn't everything. In fact, it's hardly anything. The kind of friend you are is what counts.

✿ ***ZOOEY: I have a blast when I'm with my friends, but if any of them does anything without including me, I feel like I want to die. I get so jealous I start yelling at them. I can't help it—it just feels like they don't like me as much as they like each other.***

It's a lousy feeling isn't it? Feeling jealous is worse than having the stomach flu. You'd rather throw up than feel that soon they're not going to want to be friends with you at all. Jealousy is powerful, because it comes from fear. If you look to your friends to make you feel good, make you feel like you belong, or make you happy, then of course the thought of them not being there is going to make you afraid, and then jealous. So the first thing to do is remember that you are you whether your friends include you or not. God loves you. You're special. You are still that same person surrounded by your friends or in a room all by yourself. There is no need to be afraid that you're going to lose you if you lose your friends.

If the thought of being alone does scare you, you'll want to pay extra attention when you read chapter 6. That's where you'll learn how to be friends with yourself. That doesn't mean you shouldn't want to be with your friends. It just means you can relax. You won't disappear without them.

Finally, be sure your friends don't think you're smothering them. If you have a good, honest friendship, you can ask them and they'll tell you whether they think you're being clingy. Friendship is all about sharing.

✿ ***RENI: I used to hang out with this one girl, and we were practically like sisters. But now when we're together, we don't have that much to talk about, and we can't think of anything to do that we both want to do. I have other friends now, Lily and those girls, and I'd rather be with them. Still, I don't want to hurt my old friend's feelings.***

If it makes you feel any better, that's a common problem at your age. You're changing fast and so are your friends. It's natural for girls who have been friends for a long time to suddenly find out that they are different. One thing to keep in mind is that if you're changing, she probably is too. It might feel weird at first, but just talk to her about it. Ask her if she feels what you're feeling. There's a good chance she does, and she'll be relieved that you brought it up. Of course, if she doesn't feel that way, that makes things a little harder. In that case, you might want to do the things together that you both still like to do—go to the movies, share a banana split, play an occasional game of Monopoly—but explain to her that there are other things you're going to be doing with other friends as well. That will give her the option of reaching out to new friends too. Be prepared for some hurt feelings. Yours might even be a little hurt right along with hers when all is said and done, because changes and endings can be hard. But be as gentle and considerate as you can, and keep consulting God.

Talking to God About It

Remember that God is the ultimate friend. No, he doesn't "talk" to you nonstop the way your best friend does. He doesn't call on the phone, share a bag of Skittles, or even giggle. We'll talk more about this in chapter 7, but for now, just keep in mind that no matter what *problems* you run into with your earthly friends, you never have them with your heavenly Friend. That's what makes him the perfect one to go to with friend foul-ups. Try this prayer.

Dear ________________ (your favorite name for God),

I need to talk to you about __________________________. I really like her. I want us to be the kind of friends you and I are. I want

____

____.

But sometimes there are problems, like

____

____.

Please help me to be more __________________________________.

And please help her to be more ______________________________.

And will you please be like a third person in our conversations so we'll always be ______________________________ to each other? Thank you for giving me a model of friendship to follow. I love you.

___________________ (your name)

Lily Pad

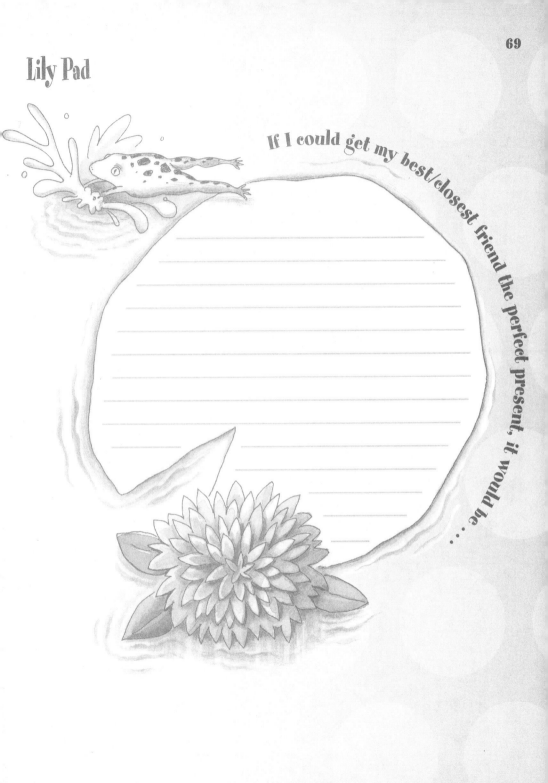

If I could get my best/closest friend the perfect present, it would be . . .

chapter

5

What Is the Deal with Boys?

"A man will leave his father and mother and be united to his wife, and they will become one flesh."
(Genesis 2:24)

Thinking about boys a little differently these days? Discovering they don't actually have cooties? Wondering what it would be like to have a boyfriend?

Or are you trying to figure out for the life of you why your friends or your older sister can talk about nothing but boys when you are convinced they're nothing but a big pain in the neck? Would you still rather have a tooth extracted—without Novocain—than have to sit next to a male creature at the lunch table?

It doesn't matter where you are on the topic of boys—we'll get into that later in this chapter. Wherever you are, you're right where you should be. There is no "right" time to discover that in spite of that gross noise they like to make with their armpits, boys can be pretty charming and interesting. But at some point in your girl-life, you *will* make that discovery. That can be an enchanting thing for you, filled with happy flirting and ribboned corsages and popcorn-sharing at the movies. Or it can be like plowing into a brick wall, fraught with the hurt of a silent phone, heartbreak, and painful disappointments. It's something you want to be ready for—and the best way to be ready is to know as much as a girl can know about these odd specimens.

How Are Boys Different from Us?

Boys between the ages of eight and twelve are different from girls their age in a lot of ways, aside from the obvious physical things. They don't play with dolls, or seem to give a second thought to the way they dress, or whisper and giggle every chance they get. There's a reason for that: hormones.

In *The Body Book* we talked about your hormones and how they change your body and your emotions at the age of puberty. But puberty isn't the only time when hormones affect us. Boys are born with their own batch, called testosterone, which eventually makes them heavier, heftier, and hairier than girls. Right now it makes them more likely to do the following things:

- Tease people, especially girls, by throwing things at them, chasing them, or pulling their hair. When there are no girls to tease, they beat up on each other.

- Slam a door when they could just close it, yell when they could just speak, run when they could just as easily walk.
- Turn everything into a weapon. A fly swatter becomes a sister swatter. An empty paper towel roll turns into a laser gun. A banana serves nicely as an AK-47.
- Dwell on bodily functions. You probably don't know one who can't burp or make other disgusting noises at the drop of a hat.
- Compete with anything that moves. Everything from finding Bible verses to getting the most red M&M's out of the package becomes a contest. Winning at sports is a matter of life and death.

Testosterone makes boys aggressive, competitive, and physical. It does not make them smarter, emotionally stronger, or more valuable to God. It's just a hormone, and it allows men and women to be different enough so that together they have everything they need for a successful life, should they decide to get married. You are not inferior because you're female. You're just different from males, probably in some of these ways:

- You talk more.
- You hug your friends instead of wrestling them to the ground to show them that you love them.
- Rather than double over in hysterical delight, you find it disgusting to hear someone pass gas.
- You like to win, but you don't sulk for two days if you don't.
- You give an occasional thought to whether you'll ever get married and have your own kids.
- You like to go to weddings.
- You skip.
- You're not disappointed if somebody gives you clothes for your birthday.

I'm not putting girls into one slot and boys into another. You may well be a lean, mean batting machine out on the softball field. Weddings may bore you, and you may be the champion burper on the block. But if you look at boys as a whole, compared to yourself, you'll probably see more differences than similarities. Even the girl who has never played with a doll in her life and would rather wear Levis than a dumb dress any day of the week probably doesn't punch her girlfriends on the arm or practically throw up when her sister gives her a hug.

The differences aren't all due to hormones, of course. Boys are usually raised differently than girls no matter how hard parents may try to keep it all the same. Boys themselves call the shots. They stop going to their moms and dads for comfort when they get a bruise or a mosquito bite at an earlier age than girls, for instance. They stop climbing into their dads' laps sooner. They usually even stop crying sooner. Naturally, they get less cuddling and hugging—not because they smell funky but because they stick out their arms and say, "Don't come any closer! I'm fine!"

Boys also tend to look at the world around them and see that, even though more and more women have careers these days, men are still responsible for supporting their families most of the time. They see that if a woman is out of work, she's just between jobs. If a man isn't working, everybody panics, and he can barely hold his head up until he gets on a payroll again. So while girls are daydreaming about wedding dresses and names for babies, boys tend to be thinking about what they're going to be when they "grow up." Whether they ever will is debatable among girls, but the point is that their attention is on something entirely different. Try to get a nine-year-old boy to play house with you and see what happens!

The problem with all these differences is that they make it so hard to understand boys. Wouldn't it be easier if boys were a little more like us, so we'd know what to expect when we get thrown into a project group with them or have to be partners in folk dancing?

HOW IS THIS A God Thing?

God made Eve because Adam needed her. It happened this way: "So the man gave names to all the livestock, the birds of the air and all the beasts of the field. But for Adam no suitable helper was found" (Genesis 2:20).

Not long after that, Eve did the first thing Adam couldn't do: she had babies. Not only did God give females the ability to have babies, he gave us the qualities we need to take care of them. By the time of the prophet Isaiah, those qualities women had that men didn't were so well known that Isaiah could use them to help people understand God's love: "Can a mother forget the baby at her breast and have no compassion on the child she has borne?" (Isaiah 49:15).

God gave women a whole slew of qualities to develop. If you read Proverbs 31:10–30, you'll find these:

- mind sharp as a tack—you can't put anything past this chick
- eager hands—she doesn't sit around and wait for somebody else to do it
- tons of energy—she goes for it
- emotional strength—she isn't crushed by a dirty look; she knows God loves her
- creativity—if she doesn't have something, she'll create it
- kindness—this is not the girl who snaps people's heads off when she's in a bad mood
- generosity—what's hers is yours
- wisdom—she listens to God all the time

God gave men some of those same qualities but threw in a couple of different ones to equip men for the plans he had for them.

- He made them fiercer than women: "The Egyptians will be like women. They will shudder with fear at the [Lord's] uplifted hand." (Isaiah 19:16)
- He made them physically stronger: "Husbands, in the same way be considerate as you live with your wives, and treat them with respect as the weaker partner." (1 Peter 3:7)

- He wants men to be even-tempered, worthy of respect, self-controlled, and sound. He wants them to be serious and full of integrity (Titus 3:2, 7–8). You may not know any boys who are like that yet, but if God expects it, then it's possible. They come equipped with the potential.

When you're thinking about God making males and females different, don't get carried away and start thinking we're from a different planet than they are. It'll help to keep these two things in mind:

- There is no religious difference between us: "There is neither Jew nor Greek, slave nor free, male nor female, for you are all one in Christ Jesus." (Galatians 3:28)
- As different as we are otherwise, in the long run, we need each other: "In the Lord . . . woman is not independent of man, nor is man independent of woman. For as woman came from man, so also man is born of woman. But everything comes from God." (1 Corinthians 11:11–12)

Your Boy-Tude

As I pointed out at the beginning of this chapter, not everybody is on the same page at any age when it comes to boys. That's as natural a difference as the differences between when different girls grow breasts and when they're ready for high heels. Just to ease your mind on that, check yourself out.

Check Yourself Out

Circle the letter of the answer that best describes you. As always, be totally honest. There are no right or wrong answers.

1. **If a cute boy I didn't know came up to talk to me at school, I would:**
   A. not believe it, because I don't think any boy is cute.
   B. love it, even if I was so freaked out I ran off.
   C. stand there and talk to him; what's the big deal?—he's a boy.

2. **When there's kissing on TV or in a movie, I:**
   A. cover up my eyes or go get a snack. I think that stuff is disgusting.
   B. watch carefully and think about what it feels like.
   C. wait for the next scene.

3. **If my friends teased me about liking some boy, I would:**
   A. smack them up the side of the head or something.
   B. tell them exactly who I like and why.
   C. wonder where they ever got that idea!

4. **If there was a girls-invite-the-boys party (and it was okay with my parents), I would:**
   A. refuse to go! What fun would *that* be?
   B. have a hard time deciding which cute boy to invite.
   C. ask a friend of mine who's a guy, but we probably wouldn't hang out together the whole time.

5. **If a teacher put me in a project group with all boys I would:**
   A. put up a major fuss or pout the whole time. I can't think of anything worse!
   B. probably never get any work done because I would want to talk to all of them.
   C. just do the work, although I would wish there were at least one other girl.

Now count up the number of A's, B's, and C's you circled.

A ____ B ____ C ____

If you had mostly A's, you're probably at a place where boys pretty much gross you out. Maybe you've come up against a pack of obnoxious ones who turned you off to the whole gender, or maybe you just haven't discovered that behind all that grossness there are some things about them that make them pretty irresistible sometimes. You are perfectly normal. Don't force yourself to endure them because your friends are all into chasing them around or calling them on the phone. The day will come when you'll find at least one who is kind of interesting, and then you'll know you're ready. In the meantime, enjoy your girlness. The boys will come in to complicate things soon enough.

If you had mostly B's, you have discovered boys and like what you've found. You might really be fascinated by watching them, or you may be itching to try your luck at getting their attention—or maybe you already have. That's normal too. As long as boys don't occupy your every waking (and sleeping) thought, it's healthy to be interested in them. As long as you know that at this age socialization revolves around just talking and being friends and hanging out with other kids, it's okay to want boys around. And as long as you know you are amazing with or without the attention of a boy, it's perfectly fine to wonder if boys like you too.

If you had mostly C's, you're at kind of a neutral place. Boys don't turn you completely off or send you racing for the Pepto-Bismol, but they don't speed up your heart rate either. For you, they're no big deal one way or the other. That's absolutely normal. Don't let anybody tell you that you're fooling yourself, or that you're afraid of boys, or that you're too much of a tomboy. You have other things to think about. Meanwhile, you're probably pretty comfortable with boys as friends, and that's a point in your favor. When you do find out that some boy is kind of exciting, you'll know how to be his friend, not just his girlfriend. That's how the best relationships with boys start anyway.

As long as your boy-tude isn't interfering with your being a happy, healthy, God-centered you, you're okay. Whether you're still running from boys like they have the plague or talking about them all night at your sleepovers, you do need to know how to deal with that boyness of theirs, because unless you go to an all-girls' boarding school, they're everywhere.

Girlz WANT TO KNOW

✿ ***LILY: I don't get along with boys at all, even the nice ones. My mom says it's because I'm bigger than they are. My dad says it's because I'm smarter than they are. Who's right?***

Neither—and both! At ages eleven and twelve, it's common for girls to be bigger than boys. Boys hit their growth spurt later. When you're in high school, they'll start sprouting up and passing you overnight. Meanwhile, a tall girl can be intimidating to boys. In spite of their loud mouths and cocky attitudes, most boys have their insecurities too, so anybody who's a head taller makes them feel shorter and less important than ever. It isn't your fault, and besides, they aren't emotionally as mature as you are either, so being nice to girls is not yet on their agenda. Now as for your being smarter, at ages eleven and twelve, a lot of boys stop achieving in school because it isn't considered cool. When they have to keep grades up to be on sports teams in middle and high school, the coolness factor changes, but right now the fact that you're still trying to make the honor roll is a mystery to them. They'll get over it. Don't change your good study habits to get boys to treat you better. It won't work. The one thing you can do is notice how you treat them. Are you openly disdainful of their shrimpiness, their clowning around in class, their food fights in the cafeteria? I'd suggest keeping your comments and your facial expressions about their lack of maturity to yourself. Concentrate on being your best self.

✿ ***RENI: There's this boy I like. Not like as in boyfriend, just like as in friend. When I see him outside of school—we both play in a city youth orchestra—he's really nice to me. We even share Cokes during breaks. But at school he either ignores me or when his friends pick on me, joins in. I don't get it!***

The key is those friends of his, honey. This boy obviously likes you, or he wouldn't be speaking to you at youth orchestra, much less sharing his Coke. But he's obviously not sure that's okay with his buddies. Boys have more of a pack mentality than girls do. We may not be able to go to the restroom without a bevy of girlfriends around us, but boys can barely make a move without checking with their friends to be sure it's cool. Only, unlike us girls, they don't talk about it. They just wait for somebody else to do it. No way is he going to go to his buddies and say, "I like Reni. What do you guys think?" As long as they're teasing you, he figures that if he stands up for you, they'll start teasing him even worse, and right now that would be like death. If you two were sixteen, I'd say forget the dude and pick somebody else. But at eleven or twelve, cut the poor boy some slack. When his group grows up, so will he. Unless it's really hurtful, ignore the teasing.

✿ ***ZOOEY: Boys can be so mean! There's a group of them in my class who always make comments about me being fat. It really hurts my feelings.***

I bet it does, and I'm so sorry. This is one of those times when I wish I had a wand to wave to make things better for you. I don't, but I can say one thing that might help: Not all boys are mean. It's just that the ones who haven't been taught not to say rude things to people are often the ones with the loudest voices. You hear them, so you think they're speaking for all boys. Read what I said to Reni about boys and their "packs." Few boys are mature enough yet to step away from those few loud leader boys and say, "Leave her alone. You're being a jerk." But rest assured there are some who are thinking it. Another thing to remember is that boys tease to get a reaction. If they don't get one, they move on. If you don't give them a response, they won't waste too much time on you. The trick is, how do you ignore a direct attack on your very person?

Try These Things:

1. Avoid being around them as much as you can, especially alone.
2. As soon as you hear a rude comment, turn to one of your friends and smile and say something positive to her.
3. If you're alone and they start in, get busy doing something else. Read a book, write or draw, stop and pick a flower—anything to keep your eyes away from them and your mind on something else.

4. Write a letter to them, blurting out how horrible they make you feel, down to the last detail. Then tear it up or make a paper airplane out of it. You'll feel better just having written it.
5. Pray for them. That's a toughie, I know, but Jesus says to do it. Everybody prays for the people they love, but it takes a real God-lover to love one's enemies. You're a God-lover, so pray every night for those who tease you. Silently pray for them every time they insult you. Go to God for them whenever you think of it.

6. Forgive them. Even if you have to do it three times a day, forgive them in your heart.
7. If the teasing gets so bad that it interferes with your being able to concentrate in school or have a good time at recess with your friends or enjoy your lunch, have a chat with your teacher. If that doesn't produce results, ask your parents to intervene. You have the right to a safe, secure place to get your education. You have a right to be treated with respect.

Not Boyfriends–Boy Friends

There's a certain point for a girl when boys stop seeming like absurd little creeps but the girl still isn't ready for romance. If some guy showed up smelling like aftershave lotion and presented her with a dozen roses, she'd probably bolt for the nearest exit. But why not have that boy as a friend?

Some people will tell you that a boy and girl can't be friends without "liking each other," without "going out." Don't believe them! A friendship with a guy can be great. Here's why:

- He can let you in on the "mysteries" of boydom before you enter the dating world; you'll be a lot more comfortable with it then.
- He can give you a different perspective on things because he sees them through a boy's eyes. Say you're not getting along with your brother. A guy friend may be able to help you see what part you're playing in driving your brother to the lengths to which he has gone to torment you.
- He knows stuff you don't know (how it feels to butt heads with football helmets on), just as you know stuff he doesn't know (what it's like to put on makeup), so the conversations can be informative. There's other stuff too—like ways to mix sodas and pass footballs and catch fish—that you might enjoy doing but have never had the chance.
- He can reassure you that you are attractive to the opposite sex without any of the scariness of "Yikes! This is a boy! This is a date!"

There are a few things to keep in mind in a friendship with a boy:

- Just let it be a friendship. Don't let yourself get all daydreamy about maybe becoming boyfriend and girlfriend and eventually going to the prom. . . .That might be in your imagination, but chances are it isn't in his, so don't run him off. Enjoy your relationship for what it is.
- Don't expect the boy to choose you over his other friends, just as you probably wouldn't choose him over your best girlfriend. Right now you're both probably most comfortable with people of your same sex. Being jealous of his other friends is a surefire way to send him down the road.
- Don't let curiosity get the best of you. Maybe it would seem to the two of you like this is the perfect situation for finding out what it's like to kiss somebody, that kind of thing. Nah. It isn't. That all comes much later. Play checkers. Climb trees. Fight over the last brownie. It's more fun.

What if you'd like to have a guy for a friend but that hasn't happened? Like all friendships, these things take time and they take God. But here's something you can do to at least get yourself ready in case the opportunity comes along.

Just Do It

Put a check mark next to each of these statements that is true for you. Leave the big space after the statement blank for now.

- ☐ I know a boy I'd like to be friends with. ____________________
- ☐ We like some of the same things to eat. ____________________
- ☐ We like to talk about some of the same things. ______________
- ☐ I see him pretty often. ______________________________
- ☐ I like his personality. ______________________________
- ☐ I think it would be fun to be around him. _________________
- ☐ I think he would be nice to me. _______________________
- ☐ I think he likes me as a friend too. ____________________

For each statement you marked with a check, fill in the blank after it. For example:

☐ We enjoy doing some of the same things. *Skiing, riding bikes, being helpers at children's chapel.*

If you didn't have any checks except the first one, perhaps you should think of another guy. This one you don't have a lot in common with, and your personalities might clash.

If you didn't have any checks at all, fill in the blanks for all the statements except the first one with things you would look for in a guy friend.

If you checked the first one and several others, maybe your answers give you some ideas about striking up a friendship with that boy you've named. Could you invite him over to play badminton if you both like to play it at church camp? Could you lend him your set of *The Chronicles of Narnia* since you saw him check the first one out of the library?

Remember, you don't have to have a boy friend, just as you don't have to have a boyfriend, or a Tommy Hilfiger outfit, or a Britney Spears figure to be happy. What you do need are good friends, and boys can be one kind.

What About the Boy-Girl Thing?

Are you twelve or under? If so, I'm going to give you my honest, straightforward answer: I think it's too soon for boyfriends. I don't think anybody's ready for that kind of relationship at twelve. So much is changing inside you—how on earth can you bring in a boy who is all arms and legs and hormones and expect to handle him and your own inner changes, along with middle school, periods, pimples, budding breasts, and fits of unexplained crying? There's no way!

Besides, most of the time, at ten, eleven, and twelve, it's the girl's idea to "go out," not the boy's. He might think its cool for about ten minutes, but he has a whole lot of other stuff on his mind, from his position on the soccer team to the video game he's going to play when he gets home from school. The majority of boys are fifteen before they really consider girls as priorities.

It's okay to wonder what it would be like to "go out" with Brian or Jason—though where you're going to "go" is anybody's guess. It's all right to glow when Brian or Jason says, "Hi," or "Nice hair." It's even fine to giggle with your girlfriends about Brian's cute dimples or Jason's crooked grin and share the dream that one of them will—yikes!—call on the phone. That's all part of the predating ritual. Enjoy it. Record it in your journal. But don't take it too seriously. It doesn't matter how mature you are or how much boys thrill you, you aren't ready for an involved dating relationship—not even with an older guy, say thirteen or fourteen. He's coming from a whole different place than your twelve-year-old boy counterparts, and you aren't ready for that. Be ten or eleven or twelve. Love it. Don't rush to be older. Don't hurry the growing thing.

So when should you start to date, if at all? That's entirely up to your parents and you. From the point of view of experience and psychology, I'd say not before you're fifteen, and maybe not even then. Some people think dating, even in high school, is just too much too soon, and why not hang out in groups and just be friends?

If waiting that long or, worse yet, not dating until you're an adult, is the most depressing thing you can think of, chat with an older woman you trust—your mom or another relative, a church staff person or a school counselor. If you're twelve and are chomping at the bit to be with a boy, chances are there's an empty space in you that you're wanting to fill. It could be something as simple as not getting enough attention from your dad. It's better to fix that than to get all mixed up about a relationship your girl-child-self isn't ready for yet.

Whatever the case, you know you can go to God with it.

Talking to God About It

Dear _______________ (your favorite name for God),

Since I can tell you absolutely everything and anything, I'm going to tell you something about how I feel about boys right now:

____

____

____

____

____

____.

When I read that over, I see that I need help with _________________.

I'm giving it to you, God. I'm going to be looking for your answers and your help all around me—in the adults I trust, in the Bible readings you lead me to, in the good, strong changes I feel in my heart and think in my head.

I know these things take time. I will wait for you. After all, you're my best guy friend!

Amen.

_____________________________ *(your name)*

Lily Pad

If I were a guy, I would/wouldn't _______________________________.

Do you have a better example? What it's like to put on makeup?

chapter
6

Getting Along with Myself

"I praise you because I am fearfully and wonderfully made; your works are wonderful."
(Psalm 139:14)

Be Friends with Me? Why?

Why be friends with yourself, get along with you, love the me you live with all the time? The best reason I can think of: because it's a God-thing.

HOW IS THIS A God Thing?

God doesn't make garbage. Seriously. His works, as the psalm says, are wonderful, and that doesn't just apply to the Atlantic Ocean, the Redwood Forest, or even everybody else. It means YOU too.

"But I'm such a loser sometimes!" you might be saying.

You are definitely not a loser, ever. You may—probably—DO things that aren't wonderful, but you're worth working on. The idea of the true YOU that God thought up and created is, well, "fearfully and wonderfully made." He wove you together, ordained your days, and put you here to be wonderful.

Why wouldn't you want to be friends with somebody like that?

If you still aren't convinced, you're not alone. Most people have a hard time really liking themselves and taking the time to find out who God made them to be. Most of us are pretty busy covering up all the dumb stuff we do and creating some other person in the process! Some of us pretend nothing bothers us so nobody will know we're scared to death. Some of us make fun of other people to make ourselves feel superior because we feel so small inside. Some of us point out other people's faults to get the attention away from our own stuff. Some of us try to be perfect so maybe nobody'll find out we're not!

That's human beings for ya. And that's exactly why God sent his son, Jesus Christ, to not only teach us how to be ourselves but so he could take the punishment for all those sins we're trying to cover up. Jesus *died* so that we don't have to hide who we are under a load of sins. Because of how much God loves us—enough to sacrifice his KID, for Pete's sake—we can take all that inner junk to him, be forgiven, and go on being who we are: the loved, cherished, wonderfully made children of God.

Have you ever watched a new kid at school? She comes in all shy, looking around to see what everybody else is

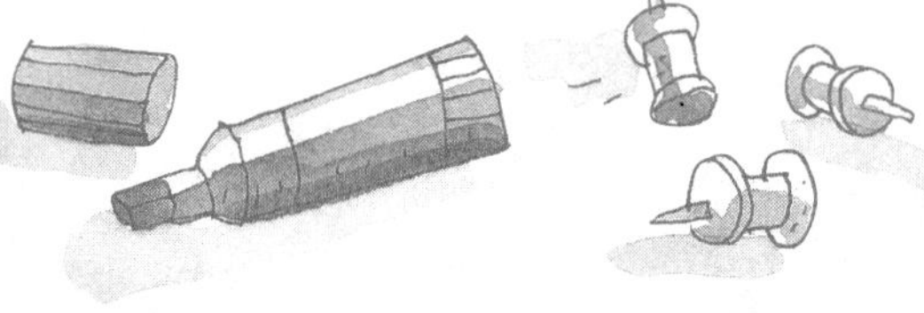

doing and acting like she's about to start bawling. Then one of the other girls goes up to her on the playground or in the lunchroom and is nice to her, and suddenly her eyes light up—she smiles—she laughs—and you find out she's really pretty fun and is going to fit right in. When you pay attention to somebody, talk to her, laugh with her, do the things she likes to do—her real self comes out and she doesn't have to cower like a whipped puppy.

It works the same way with yourself. If you make friends with you—God's kid—you are free to be just who you are. You're happier. You like yourself better—

"But wait a minute," I can hear you saying. "Isn't that selfish?" "Wouldn't that make me conceited?" "My mom says it's vain to love yourself!"

You're right that selfishness and conceit and vanity are bad news. The Bible's clear about that. Paul wrote, "It is not the one who commends himself who is approved" (2 Corinthians 10:18). Jesus himself told his followers not to be like the teachers of the law who were always parading around trying to get the places of honor at banquets.

But loving yourself isn't being selfish or conceited or vain. It isn't a matter of telling everyone how wonderful you are and pushing and shoving to get the most important place to sit. Jesus didn't say, "Love yourself *more* than you love your neighbor" or "*instead of* your neighbor." He said to treat ourselves with the same kind of love he taught us to give each other—the same kind of love he showers on all of us. Many people call that self-esteem. Since our goal is to love ourselves the way God loves us, we're going to call it God-esteem.

What does healthy God-esteem do for you?

1. It keeps you from worrying about being better than this girl or not being as good as that girl. It reminds you that God made you special.
2. It helps you make good decisions. People who do things like take drugs, paint graffiti on freeways, and drop out of school usually do so because they don't expect much of themselves.
3. It helps you know and follow God's will for your life. If you think you're worthless, you're not going to notice, much less believe, the signs that tell you God wants you witnessing to other Olympic athletes or working in a mission in South Africa.

4. It helps you treat other people better. You practice on yourself and then automatically transfer love and respect to the people around you.
5. It attracts people to you. Think about it—would you rather spend time with someone who is sure of herself and eager to take on whatever comes along, or somebody who is constantly putting herself down and is afraid to try something as trivial as a new pizza topping?
6. It keeps you from thinking that you are only worth what other people think you are worth. That sure comes in handy when it seems like there can only be so many cool people in a school and they're all in one small group. It helps when you don't get picked for the team. It helps when your mom can't afford to buy you the same kind of shoes everybody else is wearing.

Where Do You Stand with You?

Let's take a look at how you feel about yourself right now so you'll know where to go from here. Circle the answer that best describes you. Remember to be honest with yourself. That'll be your first step toward good God-esteem.

1. If I invited the most popular girls in my class to my birthday party and none of them came, I would:

A. feel like my party was ruined—and I would feel worthless.
B. pretend it didn't bother me, even though it did at least a little.
C. decide I didn't need to be friends with people who would snub me.

2. If I were invited to a party by a girl in my class who didn't have a lot of friends because she's, well, kind of a nerd, I would:

A. not even consider going; why would I?
B. either make up an excuse not to go or just go for a little while.
C. be pleased that she invited me and go.

3. If somebody were having a party and none of my close friends were going because they thought the girl giving it was a geek, I would:

A. not go; I'd do what my friends were doing.
B. make up an excuse to the girl for not going or go for a little while but not tell my friends.

C. go anyway, because you can never tell how much fun you might have.

4. If I don't do well on a test, I feel:

A. like I'm stupid.

B. like throwing it away and forgetting about it.

C. like finding out what I did wrong.

5. There are some things I do pretty well.

A. Oh, yeah, right. Are you kidding? I don't do anything well.

B. Maybe—but I can only think of one or two.

C. That's true about me.

6. If the teacher told our class to divide up into groups on our own, I would:

A. sit there and die inside until somebody picked me—*if* anyone ever did.

B. be pretty sure my friends would want to be with me.

C. go right to the people I wanted to be with.

7. If I had to move away to another town:

A. nobody would miss me here.

B. some people would notice I was gone, and some might even miss me.

C. I know I would be missed.

8. If my friends and I were deciding what to do on a Saturday afternoon, I would:

A. wait for them to choose something, because nobody listens to me anyway.

B. put in my opinion but not argue for it even if I thought I was right.

C. talk about what I'd like to do although not insist on my own way.

9. If I don't understand a homework assignment, I:

A. cry or tear it up or throw it across the room—something like that.

B. just don't do it.

C. try to get help, even if it's from the teacher the next day.

10. If I were at summer camp and had a chance to learn how to sail a sailboat, I would:

A. not try it because I know I'd sink it or something.
B. try it if the rest of my friends were trying it or if the teacher could convince me it was easy (or both!)
C. go ahead and try it.

11. If I started reading a book and really liked it but there were some hard words, I would:
A. put it back on the shelf.
B. read about half of it and then quit because I get tired of working so hard.
C. read the whole thing.

12. If I went to school with a new haircut I really loved and some girl said, "What did you do to your hair?" I would:
A. cry or insult her back or smack her—but I'd probably also hope my hair would grow back really fast.
B. go to my friends and ask them if *they* liked it.
C. shrug it off, because, after all, I like my new haircut.

Okay, it's time to count up you're A's, B's, and C's:

A ____ B ____ C ____

Here's what your numbers tell you:

If you had more A's than you had other letters, you probably don't feel good about yourself right now. My heart goes out to you, because that can really hurt. You feel like you can't do things, that you don't matter much, that you fail a lot, and that, basically, you're not worth as much as some other people. Please, please, please read and study this chapter very carefully. It's written just for you, because nobody should have to feel that way and God doesn't want you to. He doesn't make people who can't do things, who don't matter, who are always unsuccessful. In this chapter you'll find out how you can stop feeling bad and start enjoying being the person God made you to be. We're going to work on your God-esteem.

If you had more B's than you had other letters, there are some things about yourself that you think are okay, that you even like. But there are also some things you aren't happy about, and those things might be keeping you from being as happy as you could be. Please read and study this chapter carefully. It's written just for you, because God wants you to love *all* of you. He made all of you, and he wants you to discover the unique individual that you are, under all those hurtful feelings. In this chapter you'll find out how you can be confident enough to do the things you want to do, how you can get the sense that you really do matter, how you can shake off the feeling of failure. We're going to work on your God-esteem.

If you had more C's than other letters, you're feeling pretty good about your sweet self right now, and that isn't conceited or vain or selfish. That's what God wants, because you've obviously discovered a lot of who he made you to be and haven't covered it all up with fears and frustrations and other funky things. Please read and study this chapter carefully though, because as your teen years approach, you are going to experience more and more pressure to be somebody other than who you are. You want to be ready for that so you don't lose your precious God-esteem. We're going to make it even stronger.

What Does Healthy God-ESTEEM Look Like?

God has made each of us unique, right down to our fingerprints. (By the way, did you also know that every person's ears are different from every other person's ears in the world?) But there are certain things that all persons with a healthy sense of God-esteem have in common. Here's the list of evidence that God-esteem is running through somebody's bloodstream:

- She has **respect** for other people, which starts with respect for herself.

EXAMPLE: Lily gets invited to a party at Zooey's house. Zooey isn't the most popular girl in the school by a long shot, and all the "popular" girls—like Ashley and her friends—have made it public that they wouldn't be caught dead going to Zooey's party. Lily says she thinks she'll go anyway. Zooey has always been nice to her. Wouldn't it be rude to just turn her down flat the way Ashley and her friends are doing? Ashley spreads it around that Lily is as much of a geek as Zooey is if she goes to her party. Lily has enough respect for herself to

be able to decide on her own what she's going to do and not do, and she sure isn't going to let Ashley determine that. She goes to the party and has a good time. It turns out that Zooey is a hoot; her family raises basset hounds, which are so cool, and her mom makes the best double-fudge brownies in the world.

- She feels **competent**. That means she knows she can do a lot of things well, which makes her feel as if she can cope with new things that come along.

EXAMPLE: Reni is a whiz at math and science. She's a fast runner. She has a quick sense of humor, pretty sophisticated for an eleven-year-old. She plays the violin and is learning quickly. She ties great bows, is the only one in her family who can program the VCR, and can touch her nose with her tongue. The best part is, she knows she can do all that stuff, and it makes her happy.

- She knows she **belongs**. She's secure in her family, with her friends, and in her own private world.

EXAMPLE: Kresha lives with her mom and two younger brothers. Her dad died when she was younger, but she still feels secure at home because she knows how much her mom loves her. Her little brothers drive her nuts, but they also stick up for her when people pick on her. They come to her with their problems, and sometimes they even take over her dishwashing responsibilities when she has a ton of homework. She also has a small group of friends she knows she can count on for anything, and they feel the same way about her. But Kresha doesn't mind being alone once in a while. She feels safe in her room, writing in her journal, listening to her music, dreaming her dreams. Her own thoughts don't frighten her, especially because she knows God loves her most of all.

- She knows she **matters,** that if she weren't around, that would make a difference to people.

EXAMPLE: Suzy is quiet, but she is still a presence in the circles of her life. She knows her mom likes it when she comes into her mom's room and sits on the bed while her mom is putting on makeup. She knows her dad enjoys having her ride along with him when he drives to other towns to make deliveries for his business. When she doesn't get together with her friends after school, they all call and want to know why, and whenever one of them has a problem, they always come to her because she's such a good listener. There is no question in her mind that she makes a difference to the people she loves.

- She knows she can **influence** other people in a positive way. People listen to her when she expresses an opinion, and she isn't afraid to do it.

EXAMPLE: Zooey isn't the leader in her group of friends, and that's okay with her, because she doesn't like to be in charge. However, when the group wants to do something she doesn't think is a good idea, she knows they'll listen to her. She was the one who kept them from begging their parents to pay for expensive skiing lessons. She was the one who reminded everybody that they weren't a closed club and that new people could be invited in anytime. She isn't afraid they'll tell her to shut up when she expresses her opinion. It isn't as easy at home, but she's working on that.

- She isn't afraid to **take risks.** That doesn't mean she's a daredevil who does stupid things. You won't catch her bungee jumping in her friend's backyard or taking the answer key to the history test when the teacher isn't looking. But you will find her trying new things that appeal to her, things that are physically safe and okay with her parents. She doesn't miss any of the fun because she's too scared.

EXAMPLE: Reni had never studied a musical instrument before she was in sixth grade, but when everybody had the chance to take a vio-

lin class during music time, she went for it. She risked the other kids thinking that she was a nerd. She took a chance that she'd be awful at it and squeak in front of the whole class. She even faced the hazard of ending up liking it but not being quite good enough for her parents to let her continue with lessons they would have to pay for. But none of that stopped her. Who cared what the other kids thought as long as she was doing something she enjoyed? What difference did it make if she stunk at it? She'd just check that off her list and try something else. And if she liked it but her parents couldn't afford more lessons, she would at least have had this little bit of experience, right? As it turned out, Reni was *great* at the violin, and the music teacher recommended her for the middle school orchestra the next year. The teacher there gives private lessons at a discount, and her parents are crazy about the idea of her continuing to study. She wouldn't be having this experience of success if she'd automatically assumed she would fail.

- She **sticks with things** until she finishes them. When she's done, she has a real feeling of accomplishment, and that just makes it easier for her to finish the next thing.

EXAMPLE: Suzy is really good at gymnastics and dance, so when the studio where she took lessons offered an advanced jazz course, she decided to take it. After the first class, she was sorry she had. It was incredibly hard, and the teacher was really demanding. But Suzy was determined to stick it out. She talked to the teacher about the problems she was having, and to her surprise, the teacher gave her a little extra help on the side. Suzy practiced at home and paid extra close attention in class. By the end of the course, she was holding her own and had learned a lot. She didn't sign up for the next section, but she felt really good that she hadn't quit before she even started.

- She **trusts herself** to make good decisions. That means she is close enough to God and to her parents to know what's right and what's wrong. It also means that if she doesn't know what to do, she'll go to the right person for help. Once she has made a choice, she believes in it.

EXAMPLE: Lily was at the pool with her cousins, and the girls all went into the locker room. Her youngest cousin decided to hide from the rest of them and shut herself in a locker. When she couldn't get out, she panicked and started screaming. The rest of Lily's cousins split, scared that they were going to get into trouble. Lily tried to get the locker open, but it was jammed. Her little cousin begged her to keep trying and not get her mom, but Lily wasn't comfortable with that plan. So she went out and got her cousin's mom, who pried her out of the locker and then punished her. All the cousins were mad at Lily, but she knew she'd done the right thing. She still believed in her decision even though they wouldn't talk to her for the rest of the day. Besides, that night they all got over it and played Clue with her.

What God-ESTEEM Isn't

Girlz WANT TO KNOW

✿ ***LILY: I guess I have God-esteem sometimes. I feel good about myself when I do something perfectly, but when I mess up, I almost wish I were somebody else.***

You seem to like the final product, especially if it's "perfect." But I think you're ignoring how important the process is. It sounds like you do your best at everything you do. Even if it falls short of perfection, don't you think you should give yourself credit for the huge effort you put into it? Let's say you work hard on a report on France. You draw maps and pictures, do all kinds of research, and even tuck a croissant in for the teacher as an example of French cooking. You really like what you've done when you hand it in. When you get it back, you've gotten an A-. Do you suddenly like it less? After all, it's no different now than when you turned it in, except that it has somebody else's opinion on it. Good grades are important, but so is the way you try, the way you put your whole self into your work, the way you sit back and say, "Good job, Lil!" Besides, if you only feel good about the final product, no matter how good it is, you'll still wonder if it could have been better, and you won't be satisfied. And besides that, nobody's perfect anyway!

✿ ***ZOOEY: My grandmother is teaching me how to do cross-stitch, and I feel like I have ten thumbs. I get so frustrated I want to throw the whole project across the room. I'm thinking about just telling her I don't want to learn even though I really do.***

You're having some trouble dealing with frustration, which is what happens when you can't quite do something you're trying to do and tangled-up feelings of fear and anger make a mess inside you. We can't help feeling frustrated sometimes—frustration is part of being human. But we can control what we do with frustration. You can pitch the whole idea of cross-stitching or anything else you try to do and can't master right off the bat, but that will definitely limit the things you end up doing in your life. What can a person do without feeling frustrated? Watch TV? Sleep? Maybe not even those! You're going to be a lot happier if you can learn how to deal with frustration. When you feel that knot starting to tie inside you, stop, take a couple of deep breaths, and then laugh at yourself—not as if you're making fun of you, but as if you see the humor in ten thumbs fumbling with a needle and a piece of cloth. Then try again. If it doesn't work, leave it for a while and come back to it and try again. If it still doesn't work, ask for help. There is always the possibility that whatever you're trying isn't your thing, but if you find yourself giving up too often, try this. Pick out something you know you want to learn to do, and then keep at it until you feel successful, using the steps above. (And it's okay to let out a frustration holler once in a while!)

✿ ***KRESHA: This might sound dumb, but I hate the word goals. My teachers at school talk about setting goals, and I try, but I never reach them, so what's the point in even having them?***

First of all, there is no such thing as a dumb question. That's a good question, actually, and I think a lot of people wonder the same thing. The problem may be with the kinds of goals you're setting. Start small with something you know you can do. Are you starting with the goal of making straight A's on your next report card even though you know you're having a really hard time with math? That's setting yourself up for failure. Instead, try these goals: To do the best possible work I can in every subject. To make all A's and B's in my other subjects, and make at least a C in math. To not get any failure notices at midterm. As you reach each small goal, set another one a little higher. Let yourself succeed so you can see what it feels like and want to do it more and more. Even God didn't create the whole world in one day!

✿ ***SUZY: Sometimes I hear myself thinking really mean things about myself. You know, like if I mess up in gymnastics class, I'll think, "That was so spastic! You're no good at this. Why don't you just quit?" Am I crazy, or should I be listening to that "voice"?***

The answer to both questions is definitely no! Everybody has a "voice" inside that puts them down, spoils happy moments, holds them back from trying new things. Some people even have more than one, and they all get to arguing in there! So you aren't crazy—and you shouldn't listen to that voice. It only takes the joy out of what you do by filling your head with doubts. It makes you more anxious so that you probably "mess up" even more. And it definitely separates you from the voice of God, the one that encourages you and loves you and talks sense into you. So when that negative inner voice starts yakking at you, talk back to it! Cut it off in mid-word and say to yourself, "Stop it—stop it now! I know I messed up, and I'm going to try to do it again, right this time. And if I mess it up again, I'll get help. But I'm not going to listen to you telling me I'm no good!" You might feel a little silly at first, but stick to it. Give it some time and some prayer. Pretty soon you'll be shutting off those negative thoughts almost before you can think them.

✿ ***RENI: My best friend told me the other day that I put myself down too much. For instance, I'll say, "You bake the cake. I'm so lame at baking—everybody will probably puke if I make it." I didn't even know I was doing it. Is it really that bad?***

Let's not call it "bad." Let's just say it's something you definitely want to work on, and here's why. When you put yourself down constantly, people may think you're fishing for a compliment: "Oh, no, Reni, you're a great cook!" Or they may silently agree with you, and that's how they'll think of you from now on: "There's Reni. Don't ask her to make you a sandwich; you'll get food poisoning. I wonder what else she stinks at." And maybe worst of all, if you keep saying out loud how spastic you are or how lame or how stupid or how clueless, pretty soon you are going to start believing it. The natural step after that is to then start behaving like a lame, stupid, clueless spastic! Nah—don't do it. Instead, tell yourself that constantly making critical comments about yourself is a bad habit and doesn't accomplish anything good. Every time you hear a put-down of yourself coming out of your mouth, take it back. That doesn't mean you should never take the blame when something really is your fault, but even then, just apologize, do what you can to make it right, and then move on. Don't remind everybody on the planet of what you did and tell yourself you're just a big idiot. God doesn't do that to us, so why should we do it to ourselves?

So Treat Yourself, Girlfriend! Just Do It!

It's good to *do* something with this idea of loving yourself. Here are some actual activities that will help you get the idea—without becoming conceited or selfish or vain!

IDEA #1: Spend a little bit of time by yourself every day. Find a special spot and a special time when you can retreat and just be with yourself. Is there a tree you like to climb when you've finished your homework and everybody else is still studying? Can you get up fifteen minutes earlier and sit in your window? During this alone time you can write in your journal, draw, make up stories, daydream, sing, or throw tennis balls against the garage. Just be all by yourself doing something that lets your mind wander free.

IDEA #2: Look at your schedule and make sure you have at least one afternoon after school a week when you aren't involved in extracurricular activities. If you don't, talk to your mom or dad about getting a day or two free. It's fun to be on the soccer team and belong to the drama club and take karate lessons, but doing it all at once leaves no time for you to just be with yourself. God needs that time to be with you too. Make a space.

IDEA #3: Consider your activities. Are they things you like to do, or are you involved because your friends are or because your older brother or sister did it? Of course, some things aren't a matter of choice. You have to go to school, do homework, and do your share of the chores. But do you have to take that art class if you'd rather read? Is it worth it to take tennis lessons when you'd much rather be in an art class? You don't want to be changing your mind every seven seconds, but if you've given something a chance and you really aren't enjoying it, talk to your parents. It may be time for some adjusting.

IDEA #4: Gather together some magazines your mom says you can cut up, a pair of scissors, a big piece of

paper or poster board, and some glue. Go through the magazines and cut out any picture that catches your eye, that appeals to you, that seems to say, "Take me! Take me!" Then spread the pictures out on the paper in a way that you like—pictures can overlap, go in circles, be upside down, whatever you want—and glue them down. Now step back and look at your collage and see what it tells you about yourself. Is there a lot of a certain color? Is that a color you wear or use to decorate your backpack? Shouldn't it be? Did you include a lot of the same kinds of activities? Do you often do the activities you have pictured? Is there some way you could? Are several sports represented? Did you include animals? Do you have pictures of people doing crazy, zany things? Do you like the person you see represented on your collage? If so, celebrate. If not, pray about it. Ask your mom or dad about it. It's important to like yourself.

IDEA #5: Pamper yourself with some little thing every week—every day if you can manage it. Check it out with your mom or dad first and then paint your toenails, eat cookies and milk in bed, read your favorite book (for the fiftieth time) in your favorite spot, make lemonade, or take a bubble bath.

IDEA #6: Make a list of small things you would like somebody to do for you. Pick one and do it for someone else. Then pick another one and do it for yourself. Present a bouquet of flowers. Bake a batch of cookies and put them in a bag you decorate yourself. Give a foot rub. Say, "I really like you."

Talking to God About It

Dear ____________ (your favorite way of addressing God),

Wow! I'm supposed to love myself. You even said so. When it comes to that though, I need to talk to you about

____.

If I had to describe myself in one word, it would be ___________________. Would you make sure that's the word you think of? Would you help me to see myself as you do and to love that, whatever it is? I already know I need to work on ____. I know I can count on you to help me with that, but if there's anything else you want me to see, please show me. I love you. I love my neighbor. Please help me to love me too so that I can truly be all you want me to be.

Amen.

____________________ *(your name)*

Lily Pad

Things I'd like to tell myself about me. (Try this in poem form. It doesn't have to rhyme!)________________________________

Things I'd like to tell myself about me . . .

chapter
7

God–My Best Friend

"Love the Lord your God
with all your heart and with all your soul
and with all your mind and with all
your strength."
(Mark 12:30)

But I Can't Even See Him!

We know as Christians that God is supposed to be our best friend—that we're never supposed to feel alone, because he is always near. But we can't even see him! Which means:

You can't call him on the phone like you do your earthly best friend.
You can't share a Coke and popcorn with him.
You can't whisper and giggle with him in class.
You can't buy matching outfits, trade Beanie Babies, or put each other's hair in French braids.

So how do you make God your "best friend"?

Let's start answering that by looking at—you guessed it:

HOW IS THIS A God Thing?

God definitely isn't the same kind of friend your earthly friends are. Instead, he can be to you what your other friends can't be, because they're not divine!

God understands absolutely everything, because he, through Jesus, knows exactly how we feel, and he knows how to solve every problem. Check this out:

For we do not have a high priest who is unable to sympathize with our weaknesses, but we have one who has been tempted in every way, just as we are—yet was without sin. ***(Hebrews 4:15)***

God is with you any time of the day or night, any place you can squeeze into. Check this out:

What other nation is so great as to have their gods near them the way the LORD our God is near us? ***(Deuteronomy 4:7)***

God will never break his promises and let you down. Further, God is always available to you. Check this out:

For no matter how many promises God has made, they are "Yes" in Christ. ***(2 Corinthians 1:20)***

"The God who made the world and everything in it is the Lord of heaven and earth and does not live in temples built by hands. . . . From one man he made every nation of men, that they should inhabit the whole earth; and he determined the times set for them and the exact places where they should live. God did this so that men would seek him and perhaps reach out for him and find him, though he is not far from each one of us." *(Acts 17:24, 26–27)*

God has all the information (and nobody else does). Check this out:

"Praise be to the name of God for ever and ever;
wisdom and power are his.
He changes times and seasons;
he sets up kings and deposes them.
He gives wisdom to the wise
and knowledge to the discerning.
He reveals deep and hidden things;
he knows what lies in darkness,
and light dwells in him."

(Daniel 2:20–22)

We need all our friends, but we need our friend God the most, because God can be the kind of friend no one else can be—not even your parents, who love you even when you've just volunteered your mother to bake nine dozen cookies for tomorrow. You have to have God. But just how do you make friends with him?

✓ CHECK Yourself OUT

Let's start by finding out where you stand with God right now. You may be surprised at what a good relationship you have already.

Read all three of the paragraphs below. Then put a check mark next to the one that comes closest to describing you.

○ **Choice #1:** I believe in God even though I've never actually seen him or heard him talk. I also believe that God sent his Son Jesus to

show us how we're supposed to live. I believe that Jesus died to show us how much God loves us—enough to sacrifice his Son so that the rest of us don't have to die. If we believe in Jesus and follow his way and his teachings and ask for forgiveness for all the rotten stuff we do, we won't die. We'll just eventually leave this earth and have eternal life. I pray to God in Jesus' name when I need something or I'm in trouble, and I also pray at the table before meals. I go to church and Sunday school pretty often, and I mostly follow the Ten Commandments, except for keeping the Sabbath holy, because a lot of times I have homework. I don't love everybody—you can't love everybody if you're human, can you?—but I'm mostly nice to everybody. Oh, yeah, and I know God loves me, because my life is pretty good.

◯ **Choice #2:** I know God is near, because sometimes when I'm praying and I stop and listen, I'll think a thought I haven't thought before and I'll feel like it's God talking to me. Or I'll get a real strong feeling about something and I'll know it's God. Or somebody else will tell me something and it's so right I'll know it's God talking through them. I believe in Jesus, just like in **Choice #1,** and I've promised him that my whole life is his to do whatever he wants with it. (Sometimes though, I just hope he doesn't want me to do anything too hard). I go to church and Sunday school every week unless I'm sick or something, and I feel like the people at church are part of my family. I try to keep all the Ten Commandments and all the other things Jesus taught, and when I mess up, which is quite often, I go right to him and ask for forgiveness. Jesus said we're supposed to love every other human being, so I try.

That's one of those things I go to him for forgiveness for a lot. I know God loves me even when things aren't going real well. I totally trust him.

○ **Choice #3:** I guess there's a God. When somebody asks me, I usually say yes because I don't want to take any chances, but I've never really seen any evidence of it. I've gone to church before, and I think it's pretty boring. I don't know about praying—I mean, how does that work? If I asked for a bunch of new clothes, would they fall out of the sky or something? I don't think so. I also don't like Christians that much. When they find out I haven't—how do they put it?—"accepted Jesus Christ as my Lord and Savior," they look down on me and make me feel like I'm less than they are. I don't even know what accepting Jesus Christ as my Lord and Savior *means!* I figure I'm a good person, and I'm nice to people, so what do I need all that church stuff for anyway?

If you checked **Choice #1,** you're closer to God than you might think. In fact, you're so close that God is probably just waiting for you to edge just a tiny bit nearer so that you *can* hear him and you *can* see him in ways you've never dreamed. Read this chapter and study it carefully. Try some of the suggestions. A new way of being is going to open up to you, and you're going to find out that God is fun and understanding and gentle and strong and basically a hero you can always depend on. This could be the beginning of a beautiful friendship.

If you checked **Choice #2,** you already know a lot about being close to God. I'm excited for you! Read this chapter carefully anyway, because your relationship with God is like any other friendship in your life: you're always going to have to pay attention to it and take care of it. Hopefully you'll find some good ways to do that.

If you checked **Choice #3,** I'm bummed out that nobody has helped you find the *real* God. I'm double-bummed that the people who thought they were trying only wound up turning you off. Please trust me enough to read and study this chapter and to try some of the suggestions. It could show world, a feeling, a way of being you never even thought were possible, n even in your best daydream. God is everything, and I sure don't want you t miss out on everything.

How Do I Get to Be Friends with God?

I was hoping you'd ask. I have some steps all ready for you. Even if you already do some of these things, read closely and think about how you could do them more and do them better. Before we start, remember one thing: this is all up to you. God is already here waiting to do his part; you can count on it.

Just Do It

Step One: **Pray**. Remember that passage I gave you earlier? There's more to it: "*What other nation is so great as to have their gods near them the way the Lord our God is near us* whenever we pray to him?" (Deuteronomy 4:7).

You don't have to do anything special. Jesus himself tells us how it's done: "*When you pray, go into your room, close the door and pray to your Father, who is unseen. Then your Father, who sees what is done in secret, will reward you*" (Matthew 6:6).

No, a Snickers bar is not going to suddenly appear. The reward is something much better—it's a feeling that Somebody is right there all the time, ready to hear your every thought, ready to calm you down or pep you up or whatever it is you need.

Just find that quiet place and that quiet time every day. Show up faithfully, and God will be there. Then include all the kinds of prayer Jesus shows us in the Lord's Prayer. Use it as a sort of pattern or outline.

"*Our Father, who art in heaven, hallowed be thy name*"—speak to God by name and tell him how awesome you think he is.

"*Thy kingdom come, thy will be done, on earth as it is in heaven*"—let him know that whatever he wants for you, you're willing to accept, and ask him to show you what that is.

"Give us this day our daily bread"—ask for the things you really need for yourself and for other people.

"And forgive us our trespasses as we forgive those who trespass against us"—lay out all your sins—all the stuff you've done that you shouldn't have and all the stuff you haven't done that you should have—and ask God to forgive you (but be sure you've forgiven all the people who have sinned against you, or it won't work).

"Lead us not into temptation but deliver us from evil"—ask God to keep all the things away from you that nudge you toward making mistakes and messing up.

"For thine is the kingdom and the power and the glory forever"—tell God once again that you know he's in charge of everything and that he's good at it. Give up all control to him.

Step Two: **Listen.** When you've had your say, let God have his.

No, that doesn't mean a voice is going to come booming from above, calling your name (although that *has* happened to people).

It does mean that if you get quiet and still for a few minutes, God can work his way into your thoughts. You might find yourself at some point thinking a thought you somehow know isn't yours alone. Or later you might have to make a decision about something, and when you do you'll get a peaceful feeling or a strong this-is-right feeling. Or in the next day or two somebody will say something to you that helps you make a choice or makes you feel better about something you've been stewing over. Those are some of the ways that God speaks to us, but we won't hear him if we aren't listening.

Let part of your quiet time with God be quiet. Then look for him everywhere. You will find him.

Step Three: **If you don't already have one, find a church family to belong to.** In his letter to the Hebrews, Paul said, *"Let us not give up meeting together... but let us encourage one another"* (Hebrews 10:25).

Church is supposed to be a place where people can help each other not only with their problems but in their relationships with God. That can be hard if your parents don't go to church. If that's the case for you, find a friend who goes to church and loves it. Then, after consulting with your parents, ask her if you can go with her. You might be surprised—if you get involved with this new circle of friends, your mom and dad may want to come with you. It's a really cool way that God can use you.

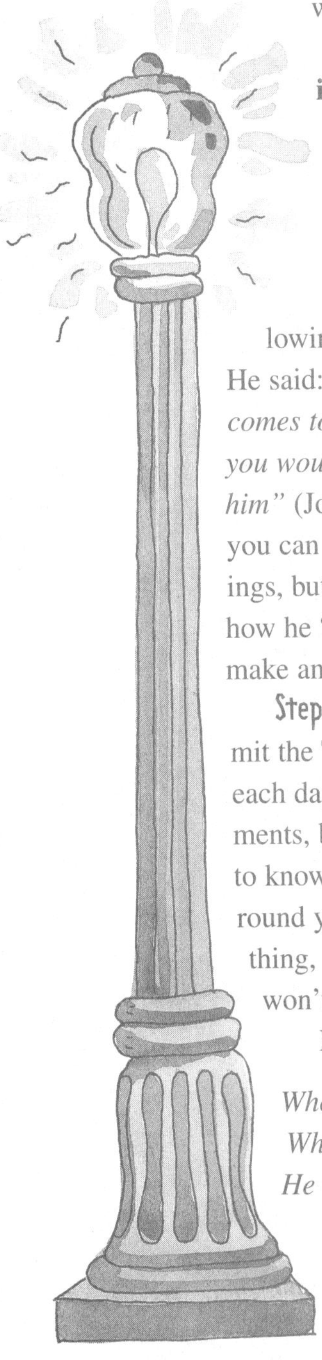

Step Four: **Get to know Jesus by reading and learning his story from the Bible.** Pay careful attention to what he taught and how he behaved. That way you'll be able to follow his example. Think about him a lot. Imagine him talking to you. When you have a decision to make, picture him telling you what to choose.

This isn't like learning a bunch of rules and then following them. Jesus said it was something much different. He said: *"I am the way and the truth and the life. No one comes to the Father except through me. If you really knew me you would know my Father as well. From now on, you do know him"* (John 14: 6–7). Jesus wants you to get to know him so you can follow his way. You'll know from reading his teachings, but you'll also know from understanding who he is and how he "speaks" to you. But you won't know if you don't make an effort to find out what he's all about.

Step 5: **Be as good as you possibly can be.** No, don't commit the Ten Commandments to memory and check them off each day. There's nothing wrong with knowing the commandments, but when you spend time with God alone, when you get to know Jesus and decide to follow his way, when you surround yourself with people who are trying to do the same thing, you are automatically going to behave better. You won't be able to help it!

How does that bring you closer to God? Check this out:

Who may ascend the hill of the LORD?
Who may stand in his holy place?
He who has clean hands and a pure heart,
who does not lift up his soul to an idol
or swear by what is false.

(Psalm 24:3–4)

Step 6: **Make the Sabbath day special.** One of the important parts of "being good" is one a lot of good Christian people don't pay attention to: making the Sabbath special. No work is to be done on Sunday, not even homework!

No, that doesn't mean don't *do* your homework! It means plan your weekend so that your chores and schoolwork are done before Sunday. None of us is so holy that we can stay close to God all the time without taking a day to really rest and quiet our minds and get peaceful.

Even the early Christians tended to ignore that. Here's what Paul said to them: *"There remains, then, a Sabbath-rest for the people of God; for anyone who enters God's rest also rests from his own work"* (Hebrews 4: 9–10).

Step 7: **Love, love, love, love, love.** Oh, and did I mention love?

No, don't stand in the cafeteria hugging everybody that goes through the lunch line. If you want to be close to God though, you have to have respect for the dignity of every one of the people he created. That means:

- no making fun of people behind their backs.
- no ignoring the new kid or the smelly kid or the kid with the thick glasses.
- no getting back at the people who hurt you.
- no shoving your way to the front of the line.
- no booing when your archenemy takes the stage.
- no having an archenemy in the first place.

You don't have to be big buds with every person on the planet. In fact, God tells us to stay away from people who are a bad influence on us. But if you want a good relationship with God, you have to want the best for all of his people and do nothing to stand in the way of that. After all, *"God is love. Whoever lives in love lives in God, and God in him"* (1 John 4:16).

Step 8: **Do it all with confidence.** Know that God already loves you, so you don't have to tap dance around trying to figure out if he wants to be friends with you too. He does! Read this scripture to yourself every day until you practically have it memorized: *"Let us then approach the throne of grace with confidence, so that we may receive mercy and find grace to help us in our time of need"* (Hebrews 4:16).

In other words, you go, girl!

Talking to God About It

Let's give **Step One** a go right now. Fill in the blanks in this prayer and offer it to God, either out loud or silently—or even in song! As long as you mean it, anything goes.

Dear ________________ (your favorite way to address God),

I really want to have a great relationship with you. The thing is, I'm feeling kind of ____.
The reason I feel that way is because ____.
The lady that's writing this book says you already know that, and that you care, and that you'll help me. So please help me to ____.
And because I'm so human, would you please help me, while I'm getting to know you, not to ______________________. I think you are ____.
Please forgive me for my attitude toward you in the past, which was ____________________________________. I'm going to love being friends with you.

Amen.

____________________________ (your name)

I'm Still Not Sure . . .

Becoming better and better friends with God is both the easiest and the hardest thing on the planet. We've covered the easy part. Now let's look at the hard things that can happen.

Girlz WANT TO KNOW

✿ ***LILY: I want to get closer to God, I really do, but when I sit down to pray, my mind wanders all over the place, and pretty soon I'm thinking about my English homework or what I could have for a snack.***

That's a common problem, and there is a really good solution. Try writing out your prayers in a journal. Try writing a poem about how cool God is, then a list of the things you are asking him to help you and other people with, and perhaps a pouring out of your confession without even stopping for commas and periods. If writing is your worst nightmare, what about drawing your prayers? God goes beyond words. He already knows what you need to say. It's the showing up and doing it that counts. Come near to God however you're most comfortable doing it, and he will come near to you.

✿ ***RENI: The other day I was really upset about something and I couldn't decide what I was supposed to do—you know, what God wanted me to do. And then this girl who isn't even a Christian said something to me, and I suddenly knew the answer. But that couldn't have come from God, right, since she doesn't even know God?***

Great question! God works in whatever way he knows he's going to be able to communicate with you. Who knows—maybe he knew that the best way to get your attention was to have it come from an unexpected source. God can use a girl who doesn't know him, because remember, he knows her as well as you. Now, of course, you have the perfect opportunity to tell her about it and maybe, just maybe, get her thinking about God too.

✿ ***ZOOEY: I want to go to church so bad, but my parents say no. They say they've done just fine without church, and besides, most churches are just out to get your money. They say if I start going to one regularly with one of my friends, the church people will come knocking at the door. First of all, is that true? And how can I get them to let me go to church?***

Let me answer your first question first. Churches do need money to operate, and part of what God asks us to do is to give back some of what he has given us. That's part of the responsibility of being a church member. However, that isn't what churches are all about. If you have gone a couple of times with a friend, maybe you could explain that to your parents, or better yet, ask your friend's parents to explain it to them. They can probably keep the pastor from "knocking at the door" asking for money. The second question, how to get them to let you go, is harder to answer. Let's start with what you shouldn't do. Don't whine, cry, beg, or nag. Don't tell them what awful people they are for not going to church themselves. Don't try to make them feel bad in any way, because in reality they're good people who obviously are doing a fine job of raising you. They probably have had a bad experience in a church at some point, or else they're afraid of the unknown, so when you're talking to them calmly and in a mature fashion, you might ask them if that's the case. A discussion of why you aren't afraid and why this is an experience you would like to have could then take place. If you show them that you aren't doing this just because you want to hang out with your friend or declare your independence from them, chances are they'll let you go. If they don't, let it go for the time being and show them that you respect their right to make this decision. Try again in a month or two. Meanwhile, do what you always need to be doing: talk to God about it. He'll find a way.

✿ ***KRESHA: I want to know as much about Jesus as I can, but the Bible is so hard to understand. Can't I read something else?***

There are definitely lots of books that will tell you about Jesus, and it sure doesn't hurt to read those. But if you want to get acquainted with Jesus himself and understand the things he did and still does, you really need the Bible. But don't despair! There are lots of translations of the Bible that are easier to understand than the King James Version. Try *God's Word For Students, The Message,* or the *New International Version.* You could go to a Christian bookstore and look at all the translations on the shelves or ask someone in the store for help. One of the best ways to at least get started is to go to a Bible study class designed just for kids your age. If there isn't one at your church, ask your pastor about starting one, or find out if there are classes going on at your friends' churches. The Bible is a rich book, and every time you read a passage, even if you've read it a hundred

times before, you'll always learn something new from it, something that talks about your life right this minute. You don't want to miss out on that!

✿ ***SUZY: My family goes to church on Sunday plus Sunday school and Sunday night worship too. But when we're at home during the in-between times on Sundays, my parents make us help work in the yard or clean out the garage. Some Sundays we actually have to help take garbage to the dump! I want to keep the Sabbath sacred, like you said, but how can I when my parents make me work?***

That's a toughie. Keeping the Sabbath holy is commandment number five, but number six, right on its heels, says to honor your father and your mother! You could start by talking—calmly—to your parents about the fifth commandment, volunteering, of course, to give up some time on Saturday to help with the things that need to be done around the house. If that doesn't sway them, you definitely have to honor their decision, but that doesn't mean you can't keep the Sabbath holy in your heart. Sing your favorite praise songs while you're raking the leaves. As you're tidying the garage, carry on a private dialogue with God about your memories of using those roller skates you're rearranging or those sleeping bags you're stashing. As for the dump, you might have to use your imagination there! There surely will be a minute or two in the day's busyness when you can rest. Take advantage of that. Instead of picking up the phone to call a friend, curl up with a glass of chocolate milk and a Christian book. Rather than parking yourself in front of the TV, decorate a binder to use for a prayer journal or make a collage of all the things you're thankful for—you get the idea. Don't forget to pray for a change of heart in your parents and to dream of the day not so far away when you'll be able to make more of those decisions between just you and God.

Lily Pad

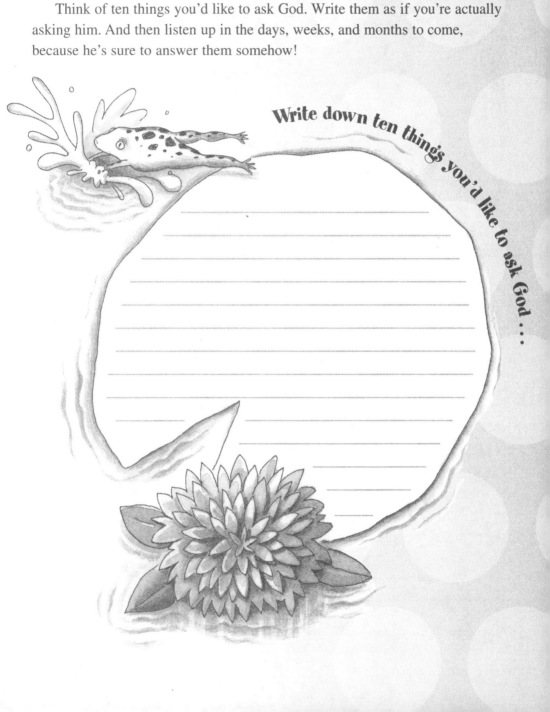

Think of ten things you'd like to ask God. Write them as if you're actually asking him. And then listen up in the days, weeks, and months to come, because he's sure to answer them somehow!

Write down ten things you'd like to ask God . . .

If you liked *The Beauty Book*, you'll love its fictional companion book *Here's Lily!*

Chapter 1

"Leo, don't let it touch you, man! It'll burn your skin off!"

Shad Shifferdecker grabbed his friend's arm and yanked him away from the water fountain just as Lily Robbins leaned over to take a drink. Leo barely missed being brushed by Lily's flaming red hair.

Lily straightened up and drove her vivid blue eyes into Shad.

"I need for you to quit making fun of my hair," she said through her gritted teeth. She always gritted her teeth when she talked to Shad Shifferdecker.

"Why can't you ever just say 'shut up'?" Shad asked. "Why do you always have to sound like a counselor or something?"

Lily didn't know what a counselor sounded like. She'd never been to one. If Shad had, it hadn't helped much as far as she was concerned. He was still rude.

"I'm just being polite," Lily answered.

Leo blinked his enormous gray eyes at Shad. "Shad, can you say 'polite'?"

"Shut up," Shad said and gave Leo a shove that landed him up against Daniel Tibbetts, his other partner in seeing how hateful a sixth-grade boy can be to a sixth-grade girl.

Just then Ms. Gooch appeared at the head of the line, next to the water fountain, and held up her right hand. Hands shot up down the line as mouths closed and most everybody craned their necks to see her. Ms. Gooch was almost shorter than Lily.

"All right, people." Lily was glad she didn't call them "boys and girls" the way the librarian did. "We're going to split up now. Boys will come with me—girls will go into the library."

"How come?" Shad blurted out, as usual.

"The girls are going to a grooming workshop," Ms. Gooch said. She raised an eyebrow—because Ms. Gooch could say more with one black eyebrow than most people could with a whole sentence. "Did you want to go with the girls and learn how to fix your hair and have great skin, Shad? I'm sure they'd love to have you."

No, we would not, Lily wanted to say. But she never blurted out. She just turned to Reni and rolled her eyes.

Reni rolled hers back. That was the thing about best friends, Lily had decided a while back. You could have entire conversations with each other, just by rolling your eyes or saying one key word that sent you both into giggle spasms.

"No way!" Shad bellowed. "I don't want to look like no girl!"

"*Any* girl," Ms. Gooch said. "All right, ladies—go on to the library. Come back with beauty secrets!"

Lily took off on Reni's heels in the direction of the library. Behind her, she heard Shad say—just loudly enough for her to hear—"That grooming lady better be pretty good if she's gonna do anything with Lily!"

"Yeah, dude!" Leo echoed.

Daniel just snorted.

"Ignore them," Reni whispered to Lily as they pushed through the double doors to the inside of the school. "My mama says when boys say things like that, it means they like you."

"Gross!" Lily wrinkled her nose.

Besides, that was easy for Reni to say. Lily thought Reni was about the cutest girl in the whole sixth grade. She was black (Ms. Gooch said they were supposed to call her "African-American," but Reni said that took too long to say) and her skin was the smooth, rich color of Lily's dad's coffee when he put a couple of drops of milk in it. *Mine's more like the milk, without the coffee!* Lily thought.

And even though Reni's hair was a hundred times curlier than Lily's naturally frizzy mass of auburn, it was always in little pigtails or braids or something. Her hair was under control, anyway. Lily's brother Art said Lily's hair always looked like enough for thirty-seven people the way it stuck out all over her head.

But most important of all, Reni was as petite as a toy poodle, not tall and leggy like a giraffe. At least, that was the way Lily thought of herself. Even now, as they walked into the library, Lily tripped on the wipe-your-feet mat and plowed into a rolling rack of books. She rolled with it right into Mrs. Blain, the librarian, who said, "Boys and girls, please be careful where you're walking."

It's just girls, Lily wanted to say to her. *And I'm* so *glad.* Wouldn't Shad Shifferdecker have had something to say about *that* little move?

Reni steered her to a seat in the front row of the half circles of chairs that had been formed in the middle of the library. The chairs faced a woman who busily took brushes and combs and tubes of things out of a classy-looking leather bag and set them on a table. Lily watched her for a minute.

The lady wore her blond hair short and combed-with-her-fingers, the way all the women did on TV; her nails were long and polished red, and they clacked against the table when she set things down on it. Lily could smell her from the front row—she smelled expensive, like a department store cosmetics counter.

Lily thought about how her mother grabbed lipstick while they were shopping for groceries at Acme and then only put it on when Dad dragged her to some university faculty party. As for having her nails done—high school P.E. teachers didn't *have* fingernails.

Lily's mind and eyes wandered off to the bookshelves. *I'd much rather be finding a book on Indian headdresses,* she thought as she looked wistfully at the plastic book covers shining under the lights. Her class was doing reports on Native Americans, and she had a whole bunch of feathers at home that she'd collected from their family's camping trips. Wouldn't it be cool to make an actual headdress—

"May I have your attention please, ladies?"

Reluctantly Lily peeled her eyes off the Indian books and looked at the lady with the long fingernails. She was facing them now, and Lily saw that she had matching lipstick, put on without a smudge, and dainty gold earrings that danced playfully against her cheek. Something about her made Lily tuck her own well-bitten nails under her thighs and wish she'd looked in the mirror before she came in here to make sure she didn't have playground dirt smeared across her forehead.

Nah, she thought. *If I did, Shad Shifferdecker would've said something about it.*

Besides, the lady had a sparkle in her eyes that made it seem like she could take on Shad Shifferdecker. Lily liked that.

"I'm Kathleen Winfrey," the lady was saying, "and I'm here from the Rutledge Modeling Agency here in Burlington."

An excited murmur went through the girls, followed by a bunch of hands shooting up.

"Well!" Kathleen Winfrey smiled, revealing a row of very white, perfect teeth. Lily sucked in her full lips and hoped her mouth didn't look quite so big.

More cool books from the Young Women of Faith Library!

The Buddy Book
It's a God Thing!
Written by Nancy Rue
Softcover 0-310-70064-7
Lily and the Creep companion

Lily and the Creep
Written by Nancy Rue
Softcover 0-310-23252-X
The Buddy Book companion

Lily's Ultimate Party
Written by Nancy Rue
Softcover 0-310-23253-8
The Best Bash Book companion

The Best Bash Book
It's a God Thing!
Written by Nancy Rue
Softcover 0-310-70065-5
Lily's Ultimate Party companion

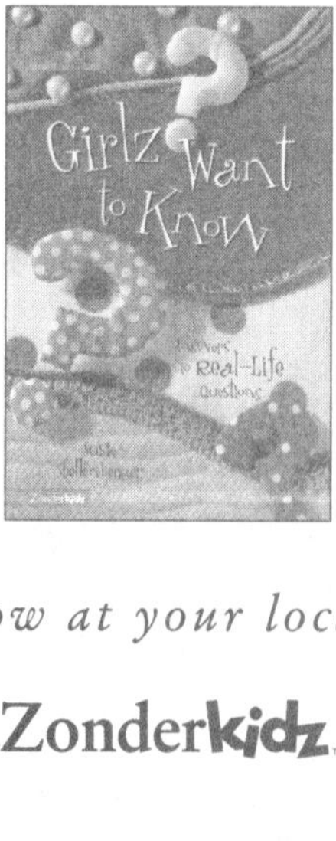

Girlz Want to Know
Answers to Real-Life Questions
Written by Susie Shellenberger
Softcover 0-310-70045-0

Available now at your local bookstore!

Zonderkidz™

Young Women of Faith
Bible
New International Version
NIV
Zonderkidz

We want to hear from you. Please send your comments about this book to us in care of the address below. Thank you.

Zonderkidz™

Grand Rapids, MI 49530
www.zonderkidz.com